ONE MEASURE
OF LOVE

What Reviewers Say About Annie McDonald's Work

Where We Are

"The characters were all fun to read about and very varied, and the plots kept me engaged as well. It was a very very fun read."—Danielle Kimerer, Librarian (Nevins Memorial Library, Methuen, MA)

"[T]his is an intelligent enemies to friends to lovers tale. …This was my first exposure to this author, and I have every intention of getting every one of her books as she writes them. If I could give her more than five stars, I would. Sharp writing, great characters, dogs, and all that food. …This one deserves 8 stars for sure!"—Carolyn McBride, *Splintered Realities*

"I truly enjoyed Annie McDonald's debut novel *Where We Are*. …There are quite a few things I love about this book. I love how Canadian the story is with a Canadian author, setting and characters. I love the bits of Canadiana mentioned in the novel such as the group of seven (especially Tom Thomson) and mentions of the First Nations stories. …Ms. McDonald mentions in her profile that she plans to write a novel set in each of the Canadian provinces and territories. I will definitely be looking for these future novels."—*Rainbow Reflections*

When Sparks Fly

"This is a slow-burn, gentle romance between Dr. Dani Waveny, and iron sculptor and hockey coach Luca McAffery. Both are well developed characters and have obvious chemistry from their first meeting in the book. I think I fell a bit in love with Luca myself. The secondary characters are equally well developed. All of the characters fit well in their roles. The romance itself is slow and sweet, with a few misunderstandings along the way to add conflict. This story really is delightful. I can't wait for Ms. McDonald's next Canadian romance novel. If you are into tender, slow-burn love stories with a definite Canadian feel, then check out this story."—*Rainbow Reflections*

"It was as if Ms. McDonald knew exactly the type of story my heart was aching for, and sat down and wrote it just for me. Add into the mix the slow romance, the secret and heartbreak that Dani carries, and the shame that weighs Luca down and you have the tale of two complex people that doesn't let go. But the characters that surround them are just as interesting, and I found myself frequently cheering for a couple of them as well."—Carolyn McBride, *Splintered Realities*

"This story is one of love, hope, change and finding happiness. It's about realizing what is important and giving yourself permission to be happy. The love story was slow-burn, but ultimately intense and hot. I enjoyed being with Dani and Luca and seeing their passion bloom. The pacing of the story worked well. We got to know the two women, and what made them tick, slowly. I thought I knew where the story was going, but the author surprised me. I loved the descriptive language, as it let me envisage an area of Canada I'm not familiar with."—*Lesbian Review*

Visit us at www.boldstrokesbooks.com

By the Author

ONE MEASURE OF LOVE

by

Annie McDonald

2025

CREDITS
Editor: Cindy Cresap
Production Design: Susan Ramundo
Cover Design By Tammy Seidick

Acknowledgments

I think everyone has a specific memory associated with food. Several years back, a show called *Pitchin' In* aired, starring celebrity chef Lynn Crawford. It was unique because it didn't focus as much on cooking as it did on how the ingredients arrived on the plate. Chef Crawford would go to locations across North America and fish, forage, or harvest all manner of ingredients and create amazing dishes with them. At the end of the show, she would sit down with the people essential to harvesting or otherwise producing the ingredient and treat them to a feast highlighting their ingredient. I still recall the expression on the face of an orange-picker as he feasted on one of Chef Crawford's dishes. He was so emotionally moved by the experience that it blew my mind. Such is the power of food. It is, I believe, a special language of love. Thanks to Chef Crawford I give greater thought and thanks to those involved in the food chain for what I am more humbly able to put on the plate.

I hope you love food as much as I do, because *One Measure of Love* is an indulgent and delectable romp through the world of competitive cooking. It required me to think about food in ways I never had. Since I've never competed or cooked professionally myself, I relied on a team of people for input and guidance, including Canada's Top Chef contestant and now successful Newfoundland restauranteur Todd Perrin, culinary expert Carolyn Power, and food writer/blogger Lindsay Wickstrom. Thank you. I'm also grateful to Miyuki Sandow, who introduced me to Japanese ingredients and cuisine.

Special thanks also go to Kathy Sano Bernard, and Molly Fisher for their attention to Japanese cultural references.

Always, I am grateful to the folks at BSB, whose dedication and hard work make everything behind the scenes possible, so that the book can shine. Thanks Sandy, Cindy, Barbara Ann, and Rad for working hard to give our readers happily-ever-afters.

And then there are my cheerleaders: my wife Sandy who makes the ideal of romance a reality; Laurie Danowski, Tam Williams, and Sandy Grimbly for the test drives and encouragement. If you have friends who you've been lucky enough to have in your life for the long haul, please remind them how much you love them. HSHS gals…I'm saying it now. Janice, we miss you.

Many Canadians dream about their favorite hockey team winning Lord Stanley's Cup. I hope you'll indulge me in imagining such a victory in this novel, but please keep in mind that it is fiction. Otherwise my beloved Montreal Canadiens would have taken the Cup home.

This is my fourth novel set in Canada, a country that is as compelling, unique, and diverse as its people.

I wrote this book on the traditional territories the Acadia First Nations Mi'kmaw (Nova Scotia) peoples and continue to be grateful for their caretaking of the land.

Dedication

To those who fish, farm, and forage
so that we may indulge.

CHAPTER ONE

S tilettos? No kidding?"

"Truth." Yaz could hear the doubt in Jenni's voice. "Pink. Satin."

She imagined the look on her cousin's face and smiled. "And a chocolate on my pillow. Dark. Lindt."

Yaz had arrived at the hotel an hour ago and was enjoying telling the story as much as Jenni was hearing it. After all, it wasn't every day that she found herself treated to a luxury hotel room let alone selected to compete in *Recipe for Success*, Vancouver's hot new chef competition. The first season was so highly rated that shooting a second season was no mystery. The real mystery was her roommate.

"Tell me more about the stilettos," Jenni begged. "What shade of pink? Fuchsia? Bubble gum? Rose?"

"Seriously, Jenn, do you think I know the difference between bubble gum and rose?" Yaz unwrapped the foil square and bit into it.

"Femme up for just this once, cousin. You know I love me some nice shoes."

Yaz knew, so she put in the effort albeit grudgingly. She leaned over the edge of her bed so that she could look across the foyer and through the half-open door into the suite's second bedroom. The stilettos popped against the immaculately white shag carpeting. One shoe was lying on its side a yard or so from the other. She took a moment to imagine it blazing airborne across the room, then another to enjoy the chocolate, knowing the delayed response was driving Jenni mad.

"They're kinda between bubble gum and rose. Maybe. Jeez, Jenn, I dunno. I see some red too."

"Red?" Jenni's voice pitched up an octave. "Where?"

"On the bottom."

Jenni gasped. "Red on the bottom?" She sounded like she was about to stroke out. "Yasu Sano, are you telling me that Miss Pink Stiletto, your roommate, owns a pair of Louboutin heels?" Another octave. "Is that what you're saying, Yaz?"

"Um, I guess so?" Was this a bad thing? A good thing? Or just a thing? It was hard to know. Anything regarding shoes beyond Chacos, Blunnies, and sneakers was truly a mystery. But not to Jenni. Nor, apparently, to her roommate.

"Do you know how much a pair of Louboutin's cost?"

Yaz pulled the phone away from her ear, her cousin's pitch and volume now climaxing. She stared at her own reflection in the screen. "Not likely. I mean, you know me, right?"

Jenni's exasperated sigh sounded pained.

"More than your knives."

"Bullshit." More? How was that possible? It had taken Yaz almost a year to save for her Shibata chef's set. How could a pair of shoes cost that much? She rolled off her bed and walked to the doorway of the second bedroom to get a better look. They looked okay. Probably better on. She imagined the pretty pink toes they would cushion, the slim ankles and sculpted calves, strong enough to pull off the stiletto height without wobbling. Not something she cared to master, but she was happy to appreciate the effort. Very happy. Jenni spoke again before she could indulge her fantasy further.

"So, who is she and why is someone who steps out in Louboutins competing in a television show? Obvs not for the money."

"I told you, Jenn, I don't know. She got to the room first and just dumped her stuff before going…well, I don't know where. I didn't see her. Just evidence of her." *Where was she?* "Shit, I hope I'm not missing a production meeting." Yaz gulped. She couldn't afford to be careless with this opportunity. She needed it. "Better check. I'll give you a call tomorrow."

"I'm on prep."

She knew this meant Jenni had an early shift at Lola's Place, the restaurant they both worked at, and would be home in the evening. "Okay, I'll try you around ten. It'll be the last call for a while. Rules of the game, ya know?"

"Gotcha. Go. Don't be late."

"Kiss Chocolate for me." Chocolate was the name—and also not the name—of Jenni's tabby.

"You're craving chocolate, aren't you? Shocker."

Yaz laughed. Jenni long ago accepted that she would never call him by his ridiculous given name, preferring to call him popcorn, or licorice, or sushi…whatever she was craving in the moment.

She licked her lips. "Not anymore." Yaz worked the foil Lindt wrapper into a small ball and tossed it on her bedside table.

With that, she hung up and headed to the foyer, where she'd recalled seeing a folder marked "schedule" on the side table. She rummaged through it and found "Day Zero—Saturday." She trailed her finger down the page. Nope. Nothing until the "Meet and Greet" at three p.m. Cool. She'd just hang out in the suite until then. Why not? It was probably three times the size of her apartment. Technically, Jenni's apartment. In fact, you could probably fit the whole of Jenni's place into one of the suite's bedrooms.

Once she got beyond the front foyer that branched into the two bedrooms, she was struck hard by the extravagance. How could people spend money on hotel rooms like this when others were living in cardboard shelters? The ghost of hypocrisy floated through the back of her mind as she recalled a childhood filled with luxurious vacations. But that was another time. She shuddered hoping to vanquish the specter, the chill quickly replaced by an awareness of the oddly warm tile beneath her bare feet as she walked into the lofted main living area.

Subfloor heating? Bougie. Jeez.

Her toes defied her moral objection and clung to the textured slate. It was impossible to ignore the dramatic décor. While not exactly to her taste or within her budget, Yaz could appreciate the aesthetic. Stonework mixed with honed wooden beams, black window trim, and matte-finished gray tile outside of the thickly carpeted bedrooms. Deeply cushioned couches and chairs with faux fur throws and fuzzy pillows were arranged around a central fireplace with all sides exposed so that even the people in the building across the atrium would have a view of its flames. Color came in pops around the room: blue bowls, yellow vases, green cocktail glasses, and red sashes tying back white-on-white brocade draperies. She laughed at herself, realizing that her mom's exquisite taste in furnishings had made a surprisingly lasting impact on her. It also explained why someone whose own bedroom window coverings comprised a ramshackle Swedish warehouse blind mended with a section of cardboard and duct tape could identify brocade drapes.

Yaz rolled over the back of one of the couches, landing prone, checked her phone, and did the math. Fifteen minutes to shower, five to get dressed. That left forty minutes to take advantage of what Jenni called a *napportunity*. She nestled into the pillowy fabric and didn't remember hitting bottom.

❖

"I love you."

Yaz stretched. It felt so nice to know that she was loved. Warm and cozy.

The sound of a kiss she did not feel echoed against the slate and brick. More of a smack or a smooch than something languid.

"I love you too, Gracie."

Gracie? Nope. That wasn't quite right. She was lots of things, but Gracie was not one of them. Who was talking? Female. Raspy. Familiar, but vaguely. Who did they love? *Wake up, Yaz.*

She cracked an eye, just enough to place herself. The couch. The nice fireplace. Yellow vase on the coffee table. The suite.

The suite! God, what time was it? Please don't be late.

She felt for her phone and found it beneath her left butt cheek. No. Not late, but close. The voices, though. Had she imagined them? She popped her head up in time to see the suite door closing. Then a tennis shoe flipped into the foyer across her mystery-roommate's threshold. She listened to a series of thumps, then detected the faint sound of the shower. She torqued herself out of the quicksand couch and made way to her bedroom. Crossing the foyer, she was slowed by a trace scent of...no, couldn't be...cookies? Yaz stopped and registered the aroma. Vanilla. Cinnamon. Soft, though. Pleasant. Enticing. Like, yes, she had to admit, sugar cookies. Or shortbread. No, she decided. Snickerdoodles. For sure. Jenni had often told her she was like a bloodhound as the two of them played the "what's that smell" game while walking through the neighborhood. Not so nice on garbage day. Jenni always lost and routinely mocked Yaz's prowess. Yaz didn't think her gift was all that strange—after all, most people had working noses—but she was nonetheless relieved that she'd gotten through the COVID years with her sense of smell intact. Maybe it was her superpower. Satisfied she'd identified the cookie scent if not the source, took another step toward her room. But as she passed her roommate's bedroom, she peripherally caught sight of a short white pleated skirt and a lavender sports shirt heaped on the floor near the stilettos. And a tennis racquet propped against the pristine white duvet.

Yaz rolled her eyes. Her roommate played tennis? Seriously? Could there be a more privileged pastime? She listed them as she stripped herself down and readied to zip through the shower herself. Golf. Equestrian. Cricket. Lawn bowling. Polo. Did women play polo? Maybe princesses. She didn't know and didn't really care. But as the water washed over and around her from no fewer than four showerheads, she wondered exactly who the show's producers had assigned as her roommate for the show's duration. Who was this tennis-shoe/stiletto-wearing princess? A princess who cooked well enough to make it onto *Recipe for Success*, that's who. *The competition.* With any luck, she quietly prayed, admonishing herself for her lack of charity, they wouldn't be roommates for long.

❖

Grace Donahue had never been late. Close, but never truly late. She'd long believed that it was a sign of disrespect—to whomever relied on you to be wherever, whenever—to be even a moment past due. Early was good. Better. But today, she wasn't early. She wasn't even sure why she'd brought her tennis gear with her. I mean, how much spare time would she have once the real competition began? She'd read in the contracts that contestants were to remain on hotel property for their duration in the competition, and that visitors were restricted to production crew and approved advisors. The only exception to travel offsite were trips to and from the studio kitchens, and the weekly outings that would give contestants access to ingredients. Both were "keenly supervised," according to the paperwork. As was internet access. She understood, but surely no one was expected to remain sedentary during downtime, and though she'd never stayed at the Pacific Rim, she'd reviewed the hotel's amenities online and packed, hoping she'd find time to hit some balls.

It wasn't the tennis practice that caused her tardiness. It was running into Taslyn Sanyal in the elevator on the way back to her room. To most foodies, Taslyn was the affable and genuinely gracious chef-owner of several Bengal-inspired haute cuisine restaurants and host of the podcast *Table for Ghee and You*. To Grace, she was Lyn. Bette's wife. Joss's mom.

Joss.

"So you made the cut?" Lyn knew that Grace had applied to be on the show. In fact, she'd encouraged her. "Not that I'm surprised. But Bette kept that secret pretty buttoned up. I'd better stay on my toes!"

Bette Kirk was Lyn's long-long-time partner and one of the show's executive producers. Grace felt it unlikely that

Bette hadn't pillow-talked. The two royals of the restaurant world had been in a relationship for as long as she could remember. As long as it stayed as pillow talk. She couldn't imagine otherwise. Still.

"You keep secrets too, right?" It was paramount to her that being picked for the show was above reproach.

"Of course." Lyn had tick-a-locked her lips as they stepped off the elevator on the penthouse floor. "Try not to worry, Gracie. The contestant picks are made by a committee of corporate sponsors not otherwise related to the show, and all candidates are anonymous until the final ten are notified and accept."

She'd exhaled and nodded. "You're right, but fair is fair." Grace reached into her pocket and pulled out an electronic key card. They'd reached her suite.

Lyn then smiled and gently lifted Grace's chin with a crooked finger. "Do you know how hard it would be to find ten chefs, even those relatively new to Vancouver, who the show's producers wouldn't have crossed paths within some capacity? Or know by reputation? Trust me, they know how to manage optics." Lyn looked at her watch, then stepped back and gave her a top-to-bottom. "Now go get ready. Bette said something about an intro meeting at three, right?"

The production meeting rooms weren't exactly what Yaz had been expecting, not that she had any real preconception of what it would or should look like, having never been involved with television aside from watching it. This was simply a nice but crowded meeting room. There was an exceptionally large conference table, and having arrived just minutes before start time, all but a handful of the two dozen or so seats were occupied. She scanned the nameplates set in front of the still empty spots, found hers on the far side from the doorway, and took her place. She tried to tell herself she wasn't nervous, but her mouth was pasty, and she wiped her palms on her thighs. Her mom's voice was in her head. "You are a Tiger. Be courageous." Yaz didn't always buy into the ancient Asian horoscope, or the one that labeled her a Gemini, but there was no harm borrowing a bit of the wild cat's confidence. In fact, it was a coincidence that her nickname corresponded with the year of her birth. She'd been given it by her parents after making an admittedly half-assed effort to learn to play golf, inspired by not only a desperate need to connect with her father, who at the time spent more time on the links than at home, but also by the then admirable golf sensation, Mr. Woods. But at eight years old, she was already a gangly height, her arms and legs growing beyond her coordination and the cultural norm. Her clubs were a poor fit. So was her patience for the sport. *Too many rules.* So, she quit but the nickname stuck.

She ran her fingers through her still damp hair, cursing its chronic disobedience, and smiled at the woman to her left. "Yaz," she said, extending her dry hand, "Yaz Sano." She thought about further defining herself. Fellow contestant? Not sure this woman was a contestant as well. Chef? Tiger?

"Kaley Abud. I'm a contestant. You?"

"Yes, me too. Nice to meet you." Yaz was about to ask if she played tennis, but Kaley's enthusiasm intercepted.

"It's crazy, isn't it? I mean, being on a cooking competition show? On *this* show?" Kaley was a ball of nervous energy, flustered but sweet. Her eyes were wide as she surveyed the room and they flashed with intermittent wonder. "Isn't that Bette Kirk? Like, *the* Bette Kirk?"

"Of course," a male voice boomed from the other side of Yaz's chair. "She's one of the producers. Makes sense that she is here. How she manages one of the city's best tables while being so involved in the show is massively impressive. Solid staff, I bet."

Yaz turned to him, fighting the urge to thank him for mansplaining. *Judge not.*

"Christian." He nodded, turning his nameplate toward her. "Brassard."

Yaz wondered if she was supposed to know who he was, because he tipped his head toward her as if she should. She had no clue.

"Brassard?" Kaley leaned across Yaz and thrust her hand toward him. "As in *Brassard's North End*?"

"And False Creek. Yes. My grandfather." He shook Kaley's hand in a way that reminded Yaz of how she handled a cut of fish she was about to dress down. More specifically, an eel. *Be polite.* She didn't offer her own hand but nodded an acknowledgement. If she was supposed to know who the Brassards were, she felt instantly glad she didn't.

She leaned back in her seat as the volume became noticeably quieter. The room was filled to the edges with just one seat left, directly across from her. Yaz craned to read the nameplate, which had been turned slightly sideways.

Gra—

❖

"Grace."

The door flew open with such speed and force that Yaz could feel the rush of air from the hallway. Out of the corner of her eye, she could see her startled neighbors lean into their seats.

"Grace," the woman repeated breathlessly as she entered. "Grace Donahue. I am so very sorry if I'm late." The room fell silent. One of the production assistants, who'd introduced herself earlier as Tiff, lifted a pen to the clipboard she was gripping and ran it down the page. Yaz watched her mouth Don-a-hue, then make an exaggerated checkmark before looking at the clock on the wall at the end of the room.

"Technically, not late."

Yaz saw Grace check the time—2:59—then breathe relief through puffed cheeks that quickly deflated to reveal dimples. *Adorable.*

"Please take your seat, and we'll get started."

As the not-late blonde moved through the crowd that filled the floorspace in the room, Yaz noticed how careful she was not to bump or jostle others, no easy task given the curiously oversized blue leather saddlebag-style satchel she hugged against her chest. She was taller than average, just an inch or so shorter than Yaz, though it was possible she was wearing heels. Her sleeveless white blouse showed off well-contoured, broad shoulders. It was only once she took her seat and set her satchel on her lap that she surveyed the group around the table.

Blue and wide, her eyes reminded Yaz of a glacial lake on a sunny day, deep and sparkling with light. They were set in a face so perfect that it made her wonder if Cinderella's artist had used Grace Donahue as inspiration. Soft edges of flawless skin, round high cheeks blushed like early apples, a classic jawline that drew the eye to plump pink lips. Involuntarily, Yaz gasped as Grace's gaze made its way around the table to her. Then Grace looked down at her nameplate. Back to her eyes. And there it was. The smile. Teeth like a movie star's. Yaz felt her jaw go slack as Grace's eyes locked on her again. Get a grip, Sano. She broke the spell enough to close her gaping mouth, but as she did, the mysterious snickerdoodle fragrance returned, wafting around her like a sweet buttery cloud. Warm. Sweet. Her stomach growled and she closed her eyes hoping to again break whatever strange magic had overwhelmed her. *Some superpower.*

"Okay, let's get down to business, chefs. I'm Bette Kirk, one of the *Recipe for Success* senior producers. The twelve of you seated at the table have been selected to compete this season. Congratulations to you all. Around this table are just some of the people who help make the show work. You will meet them all more formally on Monday morning at the studio and learn what they do and how they can help you through your time here. Today I'd like to introduce Perry Calter. Perry is another of the show's senior producers and she's going to review, briefly, how the next eight weeks will go. All the details are in the packet being sent around the table, but we wanted you to hear the highlights from us. Any questions, there's a number in the packet to text or call."

Yaz snapped back into focus as Perry Calter nudged both Bette and Tiff aside and stepped to the head of the table. She glanced around the table as if taking inventory, then slowed her gaze at Grace before looking at the clock. "We don't have many rules," she smiled as she picked up what was obviously a thick folder containing more than a few, "but let me make it clear that punctuality is one of them."

Ouch. Impossible not to notice that Perry had focused on Grace. In fairness, she was finding it hard not to. After all, Grace possessed an enigmatic quality that went beyond classic physical beauty. Under Perry's scrutiny, though, Yaz could see that Grace's smile had now scurried behind the perfect pink lips, and her apple cheeks had ripened. That wasn't fair. After all, Ms. Not Late wasn't "technically" late. And who could stay angry at such an angelic face?

Perry didn't linger—mercifully—and went on to explain emphatically and in painful detail that a television production was made up of a myriad of interconnected parts, each dependent on the other. Each tremendously expensive. *We get it. Time is money.*

"Everyone is ultimately responsible to the show's production team, its sponsors, the viewers, and each other. This is a competition intended to show off British Columbia to its very best, and you've all been selected because we believe you have the necessary skills to do just that. Every few days you will be taken to a location—a farm, a vineyard, a forest, a stream, whatever—where you will be challenged to find, pick, and/or catch a quintessentially B.C. ingredient. The challenge will culminate in the production of a dish, in studio, on the day following. That dish must incorporate one or more of the province's impressive bounty, most specifically the featured ingredient." Perry nodded over her shoulder at Tiff.

Tiff took a half-step forward, careful not to crowd out Perry. "Forget what you know about the days of the week. Starting tomorrow, we will roll through the days as our production team requires. Tomorrow is Day One of Round One. On each round's Day One, at noon, I will reveal the week's featured ingredient. Before eight a.m. on Day Two, you must send me a list of the ingredients you will need to create your dish. This list is anything beyond the basic pantry items we provide—as listed in your packages—and the ten special items you were authorized to bring of your own accord."

Perry stepped to the forefront again, a Cheshire-catlike smile spreading across her visage. "Did I mention that *Recipe*

For Success Season Two has a new twist?" Her question was obviously rhetorical. People around the table looked to each other as if the twist would somehow reveal itself. Perry was enjoying herself and dragging out the suspense. Finally, she spoke. "In light of the recent spike in grocery prices, our team has decided to introduce a budgeting component to the competition. We will set a reasonable limit based on a dinner for eight, with wine pairing. That said, you still only need to produce four dishes, one for each of the judges. You'll be held to account for every ingredient in your dish, except for those you've brought with you or whatever amount of the feature ingredient you manage to catch or find or otherwise obtain on Day Two. Be sure to read the paperwork and plan according to that budget."

The producer scrutinized the contestants, forcing eye contact. Yaz thought this might be a way of ensuring compliance, or maybe assessing enthusiasm for the new challenge. Either way, she forced herself to mimic her competitors and look happy. But she wasn't. Budgets were her nemesis. *Damn.*

Perry again gave the floor to Tiff. "To reiterate, if I don't get your ingredient list by eight a.m., our team will not be able to fulfill in time for the studio shoot the following day, so you will be limited to items in the pantry and whatever you brought or procured."

Perry put her hands palm down on the table, silently commanding attention. "The non-disclosure agreement you all signed as part of your contract with the show makes it explicitly clear that you are not to share that you've had advanced knowledge of the ingredient with anyone outside this room. No one. Am I clear? Any notes you want to keep on set are to be kept to a minimum and they will be kept at your stations but off-camera to the viewers. Understand?"

Nods circled the table. Everyone understood that blindsiding chefs in a competition show might create drama and perhaps test their improvisational skills, but it also resulted in some disappointing dishes. *Recipe for Success* was as much about showcasing B.C.'s impressive bounty as it was the competitors' creativity.

"Good. On Day Two, after you submit your list, you are expected in the lobby by 8:05 a.m. Not a minute later. You will be taken from the hotel to a location shoot. These shoots are subject to weather and travel requirements and are packed with adventure." Perry said, adding dramatically, "And misadventure." She paused and surveyed the room waiting, Yaz suspected, for an equally dramatic response. None came. Perry continued unfazed.

"With regard to the featured ingredient, there is no guarantee of the quantity or quality of what you will be able to procure. If you've watched the show in previous seasons…" she paused again, this time seemingly pleased with the collection of affirmative nods, "you know that there is a baseline. For example, if you are unable to collect even one of the ingredients, we will provide you with one. Or a portion thereof. Again, the featured ingredient does not need to be included in your budget. Read every page of the packages you've been provided with."

The room murmured unintelligibly, a mix of fear and disbelief it seemed to Yaz. Perhaps a bit of bravado as well, the majority oozing from the young Mr. Brassard on her right. *He's probably never experienced austerity.*

"You would also know from last season that even a single apple can be stretched far enough to create a winning dish. Do what you can with what you get. Understood?"

Another circle of nods. Even Yaz, who'd seen video of the show online in preparation for submitting her application, knew that the best weapon was not the ingredient, but what the chef could do with it. Within budget, of course.

Perry continued to outline the rules of the competition, regularly handing over the schedule bits to Tiff. Day Three would be spent in the studio, cooking and filming. And facing the judging panel. Contestants would not know who the guest judge of the week was until they presented their dish for adjudication. This reduced the probability that personal relationships, if they existed between a contestant and that judge, would give a contestant an unfair advantage.

"Knowing that a judge hates anise, for example, might deter someone from creating a dish with fennel. Clear?" Perry waited for a response. *She does like her drama.* "We wrap up on Day Four with contestant interviews. We have a small studio set up here at the hotel for these bits, which consist primarily of your reactions to the events of the preceding round."

"Then comes Day One of Round Two. At least, for those of you who have survived the judging panel." Perry paused and everyone knew what she was thinking. Anyone could go.

After a long moment, presumably to allow the unspoken to penetrate the contestants' psyche, Tiff launched into what Yaz considered the small print: a level of detail that quickly became excruciating. Social hour tonight at the rooftop bar. Dress casual. Sequestering, including the surrender of personal phones and other internet-access devices, to begin tomorrow—aka Day One—before the first ingredient was announced. Hotel services. Contact extensions for production staff. Judges for the season. One guest judge per round, a surprise. Read your information packet. Don't miss deadlines. *Yada yada yada.* Fortunately, Yaz's propensity for distraction and low threshold for minutia hadn't caused problems to date. She'd made it through her apprenticeship with barely a glitch. That was something. Looking around the table, though, she wondered if she needed to make a change. Grace had pulled a lined legal pad out of her satchel and, fancy-looking pen in hand and attentive to every word Tiff was saying, she began taking copious notes. Kaley was making the odd note in a small ringed notepad with a severely chewed No. 2, and Justin...nope, Christian...was presumably thumbing notes on his phone, more than occasionally glancing at the power players around the room. Yaz felt no such compunction; she didn't watch much TV beyond what happened to be on during prep at the restaurant, so if anyone in the room was special by celebrity measure, she'd have very little hope of recognizing them. And very little interest. She was here for one reason, and if energy was to be spent, it would be on defeating the eleven other contestants seated around the table. They looked like they all wanted to win as badly as she did. But budgets and time—specifically Days One through Four, would tell.

CHAPTER TWO

The contestants left the meeting room and moved like cattle into the freight-sized elevator, leaving the producers and crew to talk about "scheduling," or what Perry referred to as "the law."

"I can't imagine what goes into putting together this kind of thing," Kaley said, "And I can't believe we're part of it! This is the coolest thing I've ever done." Emphasis on "the coolest."

Yaz's first impulse was to roll her eyes, until she remembered what Jenni had said when she was selected. "Leave the judging to the judges." Yaz knew it wasn't meant as harshly as it sounded, but her cousin was right. In addition to being extremely stubborn and short-tempered, she was, admittedly, judgy. Much of the time, criticism was directed toward herself. *Mostly*. As it was, Kaley's enthusiasm was genuine and sweet, so she smiled and nodded, then took quick inventory of the others as they filed into the car. Brassard was thumbing his phone. Again. Or still. Whatever. Grace was taking floor requests, pressing each of the squares until Four through PH were lit.

"Is anyone nervous about getting the core ingredient?" A tall brunette in one corner raised her hand as if in an auction. "Hi, I'm Rhonda by the way."

"Rico," came a deep voice from the back. "Not too nervous, no. Remember last season, how that one contestant ended up with a single apple? She made the most spectacular handblown sugar apples..."

"...filled with Calvados maple crisp mousse! Yes! I still dream about it. Francine. Bonjour!"

"Hi, Francine. Me too. I'm Vij. The pantry really saved her ass. If it hadn't been for the dried apples and apple sauce, well..." he nodded, "it was still an impressive dish."

Yaz felt a bit like she was walking on thin ice, not sure how familiar she wanted to get with anyone given that it was a competition. But being a dick wasn't her style either. "I'm Yaz. Hey."

"Hi all, I'm Grace."

Brassard pushed, "We know who you are," through his teeth, eyes still on his phone—*passive-aggressive little shit*—before declaring himself, "Christian Brassard. And we were picked because they expect we can do better."

"Well, I'm not sure I can blow glass, but I'll give it a go if I need to. I'm Sean." He filled most of the center of the elevator. "Anybody wanna watch the game tonight? Before the shindig on the roof? I'll be in the lobby bar at five."

The pivot in conversation was abrupt—acceptably so—because you'd have to be living under a rock not to know that the Canucks were on a roll, and Vancouver was bubbling with excitement. Even Yaz knew that the hockey team was due for success after an excruciatingly long playoff drought, and she hadn't seen a game since she was a kid and her dad had season tickets. Several voices sounded "I'm in," or "see you later," as the floors claimed their residents. Christian was the last, leaving them with a questioning look as the Five square went dark. Only Yaz was left. With Grace.

"Penthouse?"

A pause. Then an elongated "Yeeess" with a hint of a question mark at the end.

"Pink shoes?"

Grace looked down, perplexed, then lifted her chin and tilted her head. "Yes." No question mark.

"That was weird. What I just said." *Awkward.* "Pink shoes." *Repeating yourself doesn't make you less crazy. Take a breath. Or not.* "Uh. Sorry. I, er, noticed them earlier. In the room. Your room." *Stalker much?* "I mean, your door was open. I could see them. From the foyer. I, uh, didn't go in your room." Yaz shook her head emphatically. "I just…they're nice. The shoes, I mean. Pink. Nice." *And again, that could not have been more awkward.*

Grace put her hand on Yaz's arm. "Thanks." And then the smile. The Margot-Robbie-as-Barbie smile. And cookies. Again with the snickerdoodles.

"I'm Yasu…Yaz Sano. I guess I'm your roommate. Suitemate." *Gaaaa.* "Is it weird that we're in the penthouse? I'm not complaining, I mean, it is swank."

Vertical creases formed above the perfect nose. "It is, yes. Both weird and swank." She pulled her key card out of her blue bag and waved it in front of the door lock. "It's a boutique hotel, so it's possible that all the suites are like ours." Her tone was dubious, and the creases hadn't ebbed.

Yaz followed her into the foyer and the sweet scent of snickerdoodle wafted around her. Designer air freshener, maybe? Part of the swank experience?

"Will you be going to the lobby? For the game?"

"Oh, uh, not sure. I need to do a bit of inventory before they shut down our internet access." Grace tossed her bag like it was a cornhole biscuit toward her bed. It caught the edge and landed with a thud on the rug near the stilettos. "Darn! So close!" She laughed. And snorted. But cutely.

"Saving your ringers for in the kitchen?" Yaz was hoping for another endearing snigger, but instead Grace exhaled nervously.

"Good lord, I can only hope that by the time we're in the kitchen I've got my mind right. All I can think about right now is keeping my business afloat while I'm here."

"What do you do?"

"I own a pie shop. It's a pop-up of sorts. I mostly supply cafés and diners. Small-scale." Grace went to the kitchenette and took two glasses from the cabinet, then filled them with water from the countertop dispenser and handed one to Yaz.

"Thanks." Their fingers touched in the exchange and Yaz noticed it far too much. "So you have a staff? To look after things while you're here?"

"Not exactly. A part-time staff of one. She's a student from the culinary arts program at Vancouver Community College. Emily's just going to receive deliveries and do some basic prep work until I'm back. I don't really need her help since the storefront is closed, but she needs the income for school."

"That's nice that you look after her." Yaz meant it. She remembered her own school days very clearly because her debt still followed her. And she was sacrificing a lot to be on the show. She wouldn't be paid, so this was a huge risk. But she was as prepared, culinarily, as she'd ever been. She had Sabrina to thank for that. Hopefully, she'd be able to put at least her debts to rest if she could pull herself together and win *Recipe for Success*. But that wasn't going to happen if she was distracted, and Grace Donahue, with her cute little laugh, adorable dimples, perfect fingers, and unflappable niceness was a temptation she needed to shut down. "Speaking of looking after, I've got a few things I need to do before the rooftop gig." *That was a bit of a lie.* "So, I'll see you up there later?"

"You bet. Oh, and, Yaz?"

She stopped and looked back over her shoulder. "Yeah?"

"I just wanted to say that I'm looking forward to kicking your butt in the competition," she winked and, yep, smiled that smile, "but I'm happy you're my roommate. See you later!"

Game on, Grace Donahue, game on.

CHAPTER THREE

Yaz filled the hour before cleaning up for the soiree—which amounted to washing her face and wrangling her cursed hair into something that looked less like a helmet—by reviewing some of her school notes, and those she'd attentively scribbled down while working with Sabrina at Safe Harbor, the local soup kitchen. Sabrina Marline had been, well, was still the best chef she'd ever worked with. Life had dealt her some truly shitty blows, but she had found her feet and fortunately for Yaz, had decided that sharing her wealth of knowledge was her latest mission. Along with cooking for over a hundred people sleeping rough in the city's downtown east side, Sabrina set aside time each week to walk Yaz through techniques that she either hadn't learned in school or encountered at her job.

Her job. Not exactly chef de cuisine. Barely a chef de parti. No one cooked below or beside Yaz on the line at Lola's Place. It was a medium-sized operation that served a variety of dishes to a variety of clientele. The food was good, though, at least good enough to help get her application to the show noticed. Lola's husband, the executive chef, wasn't a sharer so Yaz was especially grateful for Sabrina's big-heartedness. The notes were jammed into a ratty-looking canvas shopping bag but were organized and detailed. Mostly illustrated. Visual learning was her style, always had been. Her mom was the same. *Mom. Right.* Yaz made a quick mental note to call her tomorrow before the phones were seized. Early morning, before her mom went to bed at midnight Tokyo time.

Yaz temporarily lost herself in a gastronomical world of emulsification and deconstruction so by the time she made it to the rooftop, everyone was clustered and engaged in conversation. Near the bar, Vij and Sean were staring at a cell phone, beers in hand. The game, she guessed, had gone into overtime. Rico and Rhonda were standing surprisingly close to each other and to the edge of the terrace, presumably watching the sun set beyond English Bay. Or maybe oblivious to it. Maybe they already knew each other. The industry moved constantly, as did its people, and the likelihood of crossing paths wasn't unimaginable.

"Yaz! Over here!" Kaley was part of a larger group that looked to include the remaining contestants and production crew. At its center, Yaz could see as she approached, was Grace. She was asking questions of everyone, inviting them to share their stories, responding with genuine interest, and pulling even the shy ones into the light. They all hovered around her like bees, waiting for more of their queen's sweetness.

"Yip Kew, tell us about working with Johanna DeBryn! Is she as spectacular as I've heard?"

The to-this-point-silent-contestant straightened, and his face brightened with rosiness. "Oh, yes! She is a taskmaster, but the sauces! Oh, my. I am honored every day to be in her kitchen. And please just call me Kew."

"Francine, are you hoping for something specific for our first ingredient?" Grace raised what looked like a glass of bubbly toward her as she asked. Francine responded in kind.

"Je ne sais pas…I don't know," she pivoted, "perhaps a nice foie gras, though I'm not sure it's a particularly B.C. ingredient."

"We can hope though," chimed in Sean. "It's something my food truck crowd could learn to love!"

"Yes, but let's keep in mind the budgets." Perry's interjection brought the convivial mood to a screeching halt, reminding everyone that the competition was paramount.

Kaley wasn't ready to let go of the balloon. "Grace, tell us about your place. Let 'Em Meat Pie…isn't that the greatest name, you guys?"

The hive buzzed with a chorus of ahhhs and titters.

"Thank you so much. I love a good pun. And a good pie. Which I hope I make."

"Oh, you do! I've picked one up on occasion. So good!" Kaley was almost vibrating with delight.

Grace deflected by asking more questions about where people were from, where they cooked, and what their favorite dishes were. Yaz wondered if she'd eaten everywhere in Vancouver because she had specific knowledge of more than a few top restaurants.

By this point, even the servers were in orbit around Grace, barely waiting for her to finish a glass of prosecco before topping it off. Providing a fresh cocktail napkin. A shrimp hors d'oeuvre. Yaz, on the other hand, felt as though she was stalking the food trays as they made the rounds. Jenni always teased her about being perpetually hungry. But really, she couldn't be blamed. The hotel's catering was well above par. Maybe it would be easier if she, too, was a cute blonde clearly comfortable and in command of luxury. But was that what she wanted? To have *that* life? Instantly, she felt guilty. Her work at the soup kitchen had exposed her to a level of inequity, a cold and harsh poverty that even she hadn't experienced personally. At times, it was overwhelming. That's usually when Sabrina would pull her aside and remind Yaz that just because others have not, doesn't mean you can't enjoy what you do have. Especially if you put some energy into pulling others up with you. "You can't save a drowning person by jumping in the water with them," Sabrina cautioned her, stressing the importance of self-care. Burnout was endemic in volunteerism.

Yaz moved from the circle, distance needed to keep her from eating every single crab puff that made the rounds, and to break the Grace spell. Perry was right. This was a competition. Part of her also wanted to avoid any attention drawn to her own modest résumé. And her, by comparison, social awkwardness. She was looking down at the cherry trees, the remnant fallen blossoms now blowing in wispy waves down Comox Street toward English Bay, when she felt a presence at her elbow.

"She's something isn't she?" It was Brassard. His note was as sour as the old-fashioned he held in his small hand.

"In a way, I guess," she replied cautiously, noticing for the first time how short he was. At 5'11", Yaz felt like a giant most of the time. She was by far the tallest in her family. Other than some good-natured teasing and numerous wide-eyed stares especially when—at age fourteen—she'd visited family in Japan, her height hadn't been an issue. Her tomboyish style choices seemed to cause strangers more unease than her stature. But next to Brassard, she felt like a lean Yogi to his Boo-Boo.

"I don't know why she's here. I mean, her life is pretty much golden. I'm doing it for profile, for my family's business, but Grace? The Donahues don't need the profile. Or the cash, that's for sure." He looked to her for agreement, but Yaz feigned disinterest. The little bear persisted. "I guess that's how she scored the penthouse. Makes sense, I guess, given her family. I can see why my folks encouraged me to ask her out. They were regulars at our restaurants." Resentment oozed from the tiny man. Yaz wasn't sure what exactly he was suggesting, but nonetheless bit back her first thought, which would've reminded Brassard pointedly of his own privilege. Her second thought was whether Grace would've said yes if he'd asked. *That would be disappointing in many ways.*

To her relief, she was rescued by a toast that Bette King was making to the group, thanking the contestants and the crew in advance for what she expected would be another successful season. Yaz moved gratefully toward the partiers.

"To *Recipe for Success*. May we all remember over the next month or so what the ever-ubiquitous 'Unknown' once declared about cooking: it is love made visible."

CHAPTER FOUR

Round One, Day One

Grace loved the early mornings. Over coffee, she'd typically do the day's books for the shop, assign Emily her prep, and plan the menu, which took most of her time. She accepted that when it came to food, she was not exceptionally creative, so she'd settled on meat pies as the product for her business. They were a classic staple; creativity wasn't expected. Steak and mushroom pie was, well, just that. Furthermore, and maybe more importantly at this point in the business cycle, pies played nicely on the balance sheet. People were willing to pay for a good meat pie, and not many people wanted to take the time to make it from scratch. One of her biggest customer bases was in Victoria, a historical British colony still firmly reflected in the city's restaurant fare.

"I'm surprised you haven't moved there," her mom once commented, her sincerity questionable.

Grace had thought of it, but the rents were untenable, at least until she paid off her debts. Entirely. She wasn't about to share any of that, or much of anything really, with her mom. Or dad. Not anymore. That bridge was still smoldering. So, this morning she put time into catching up on correspondence, placing orders and, once done, called the front desk to book court time at the hotel dome for later this afternoon. That would be a nice reward, assuming she had her ingredient list completed. *What would the first featured ingredient of the competition be?* She knew she was going to have trouble surrendering her laptop but hoped that her careful preparations with her Let 'Em Meat Pie vendors and customers would make for a seamless re-opening when her time on the show ended. Which, she hoped, would be no fewer than twenty days from today.

Yaz, she noticed, was up early as well. She hadn't seen her but could tell from the coffee station in the room that a cup had been brewed. Fruit and pastries from the platter that room service delivered while she was in the shower had also been partially liberated. She gathered from the voices she could hear through the closed door that Yaz was on the phone with someone. The one-sided conversation ping-ponged between English and Japanese, with laughter interspersed frequently. Grace enjoyed the laughter. To this point Yaz had seemed friendly enough, but very guarded. And a bit awkward. She couldn't have been cuter about the pink shoes. Grace recalled how she'd repeatedly pulled on the odd strand of hair that fell from the spikey upsweep atop her head, and looked down at her feet, cheeks pink and teeth pulling at her lower lip. Not shy, just flustered. Maybe self-conscious? Even then, though, Yasu Sano had a presence. She'd noticed it yesterday in the boardroom when she'd first caught her eye. For a second, until Yaz had quickly—almost too quickly—looked away. Not before a flash of what? Recognition? *Do I know her from somewhere?* Not school. Tennis maybe? Shapely muscled shoulders. Maybe. Handsome, definitely. Dark almond-shaped eyes that even in that brief glance penetrated hers. Grace had found herself involuntarily drawn to a wide, sensual mouth that tapered to a small chin and long slender neck. And she couldn't ignore the strong upper jawline that seemed to clench whenever her brow furrowed, as it seemed to whenever she cast a glance at certain other competitors. Still, it had been hard to know what she was thinking. Maybe Yaz had been a customer? After all, besides tennis, work was pretty much her whole world. Until now. This competition was a diversion. Welcomed by her. She hadn't mentioned it to her parents. Her mother would be mortified, apoplectic even, and her father would be the worst kind of helicopter parent. Fortunately, she had inherited her grannie Jean's work ethic and independence. She was proud to be in the service industry. She loved her work. Most of the time. She got to meet great people. Hardworking people. And then there were people like the Brassards. There'd been a moment the night before, at the soiree, when she'd noticed the heir apparent chatting with Yaz. Especially next to him, Yaz had looked downright confident, commanding even, dressed in a perfectly pressed white shirt and green jacquard retro tuxedo jacket, with a pair of faded cuffed black jeans and well-worn dark green Blundstones. In comparison, Christian wore shortness like a certain French general. She'd met many like him. Hell, she'd dated one just like him. Back when she dated. Back when she couldn't say no to well-intentioned friends. Or her parents. Way back. She'd wondered what he and Yaz might have in common, beyond the competition. Possibly nothing. *Hopefully nothing.* Christian Brassard was part of her past, and she preferred to keep it that way. Yaz, on the other hand, was a true breath of fresh air, and from where Grace was sitting, seemed in many ways his superior.

❖

"Yes, I just got off the phone with Mom. She said to say 'Hello, Jenni Penny!'" Yaz did her best impersonation of her mom, who loved to tease her niece. Nicknames, almost exclusively good-natured in Japanese culture, were common with close relatives and friends. This one, meant to tease Jenni about her fierce opposition to Canada's removal of the copper one-cent coin from its currency, also fitted her shiny disposition and had stuck.

"Okaasan! I love her. Did you ask how Auntie Miyuki is doing?"

Auntie Miyuki was the older sister of their moms, and was one of the reasons why Yaz's mom had gone back to Japan. "Very well, it seems. Auntie's chemo is over, and she's recovering quite well. Enough that she's driving Mom crazy. It sounds like both could use a break from caretaking."

"You're going to miss talking to her for the next few weeks. Hopefully, how many again?"

"Around five weeks. I guess it's somewhat dependent on weather for the outdoor shoots."

"Don't worry, Yaz, I'll keep an eye on your peeps. Speaking of peeps, the new bartender started at Lola's last night. Her name is Carla. By your standards, I think she's pretty hot."

"Jenni, don't start." Her cousin was always trying to set her up as if it were her sole mission in life.

"I know, I know. You're not interested. You don't have time. Blah, blah. Who is it I talk to about having your 'girl on girl' card revoked? And don't tell me that your super butchy hair and your tattoos and your Tegan-and-Sara-and-The Beaches-heavy playlists are enough to keep your membership active. One-night stands could tide you over, you know, if a relationship isn't what you're looking for. You're hot too, in that way that Simu Liu is hot. You know what I mean? Cool. Aloof. But friendly. And handsome."

Yaz cringed with embarrassment, surprised at how Jenni saw her. Her self-awareness paled. Truth be told, Yaz didn't know what she was looking for, either. Or if she wanted to look. The hours and weekends and evenings demanded by her job made it difficult to maintain relationships with people not in the industry. She'd exhausted her immediate circle of contact. The organic vegetable producer who supplied Lola's. Very nice but into a few practices Yaz was not. She'd called them *unadulterated*. Yaz didn't have words. Except no thanks. Then there was a bike courier from Order Up who delivered more than a few surprises…but to a few too many people.

"If nothing else, cousin, you'll love Carla's ink. It's ultra-femmie." Jenni was working extra hard. "And unlike you, she doesn't keep her tats hidden beneath her sleeves. She has this vine that wraps around her wrist and down her thumb. Nice work."

Yaz loved tattoos. It was one of her guilty pleasures, and the one she had was private to most in her circle because she typically kept it concealed. She knew Jenni wouldn't give up and decided that it was best to capitulate. "Maybe when this all wraps up." *Noncommittal. Good.*

"I'll hold you to that. Anything more about Ms. Pink Shoes?"

"She's uber rich. And she plays tennis. And yes, before you ask, she is hot." Yaz had surprised herself by noticing, let alone sharing. But Grace was hot by all objective measures. Her face. Her hair. Her body. The way she moved. And spoke.

Those eyes, though. If Yaz could swim, she'd gladly spend a day in their deep blue.

"Anything you want to tell me?" Jenni barely contained the nudge-nudge-wink-wink tone from her question.

"Give Dots a belly scratch for me."

"Yeah, I get it. You want some twisted pretzels. Delicious, but not a morning food. Seriously, Yaz, is there anything else you want to tell me about your roomie?"

"Just that it'll be nice to have the suite all to myself when she loses. And you're wrong about Dot's pretzels. They're a twenty-four-hour snack for sure."

Yaz couldn't have been happier to hear the knock coming from the foyer. She jumped from the bed and bid a quick good-bye to her cousin, pocketed her phone, and took a split second to check her hair before racing to answer the door.

❖

As Grace had expected, it was Tiff. Yaz led her into the suite.

"Nice digs!" She took in the full 360 from the middle of the living room. "A view of the park. And the inlet. Very nice."

Yaz followed and plunked herself on the couch. She looked quite at ease, not at all the jumble of nerves that knotted inside Grace. Tiff consulted her clipboard and smiled before looking up.

When she did, she looked much happier than she had at yesterday's meeting. "Good morning, Grace."

"What's the good news?" Yaz asked.

Grace knew that Yaz was asking about the ingredient for the challenge, but she couldn't help herself. There was something about the penthouse that didn't ring true. "Hello, Tiff. I imagine," she said, ignoring Yaz's query, "that everyone's room is just as sensational, no?"

Tiff laughed a quick, "No."

I knew it! "Well, I wonder if there was some mistake in the room assignments."

"If I were you, and if it *was* a mistake, I'd be happy and just keep quiet about your luck. The other rooms are great, but this? Well…"

"It's swank, right?" Yaz smiled. Tiff nodded. Grace clenched her teeth.

"Would you like to know what Round One's mystery ingredient is?" Again, Tiff smiled as if the secret was eating her alive.

Grace perched on the arm of the couch and set aside the irritation that burred beneath her regarding the suite. She would deal with it later. "Absolutely."

Yaz leaned forward on the couch, elbows on knees.

"Canada's official national vegetable…" Tiff paused, clearly for dramatic effect. Grace rooted through her mind, hoping that she'd squirreled away the answer, but it was obvious after a silent moment that neither she nor Yaz had a clue. "Rhubarb."

"What?!" they said in unison.

Tiff was enjoying herself. "That's right. We have a national vegetable, and it grows in abundance all over the country but especially here in British Columbia."

"Wait. Did you say vegetable? Isn't it a fruit?" Grace was in disbelief.

"It is not, though most think it is because we tend to see it paired with fruits, especially strawberries, most of the time.

I can see that you don't believe me but let me introduce you to the second of this morning's surprises." She reached into a large satchel she'd carried in and pulled out two rectangular boxes and handed them each one. "In here you will find a tablet. In exchange for your phones and any laptops or tablets you may have brought with you, you will have the use of this tablet including internet connectivity, for an hour after I leave this room. There are no email or communication functions available. It is remotely supervised and will shut down after that hour. Use it for wine parings. Or research the humble rhubarb. Take notes. Prepare for Day Three, cooking day. Judging day."

Grace and Yaz wordlessly tore open the boxes as soon as Tiff had gone.

"This is sweet." Yaz was already running her fingers across the screen, tapping, swiping, and resizing pages. "Do you mind if I work on the couch?"

"Not at all. I'll take the kitchen table if that's okay. But I have a call to make first."

"No phones, remember?"

"I just need to call the front desk. We're allowed hotel services. Do you need anything?"

"Naw, I'm good. Gonna dig into some rhubarb. Canada's national vegetable? Sheesh! Remember, you only have an hour!"

The tablet was a great surprise. But the whole penthouse issue still niggled at her. It didn't seem fair. And in Grace's world, when fairness felt in peril, there was one person likely at the helm. Her father. She couldn't call him—wouldn't, really—but she needed to find a way to level the field. Unless everyone had a penthouse, it wasn't right that she did. She sat on her bed, picked up the phone, and hit the guest services symbol. To her dismay, she was told that the hotel manager, Mr. Barney, was not available until Monday. Tomorrow. Okay, this would wait.

For now, she would focus on a singular thought. One she never expected. Bring on the rhubarb.

CHAPTER FIVE

Round One, Day Two

The hotel lobby was madness. A herd of cats. Grace, marveled as Tiff deftly corralled them all onto the large passenger van. Each contestant had been provided with a pair of wellies and it looked quite comical, really. *Cats in boots.*

"I don't need to remind anyone it's eight o'clock, do I," she barked as the last of the group, Sean, stepped aboard. "And I hope you had breakfast. We'll be back well after lunchtime and there will be no drive-throughs on the way back, so don't ask."

No worry there, thought Grace. This morning the continental breakfast had been replaced by full-on fare that included eggs benny, grilled tomatoes, and pan-fried potatoes. Though she was more of a granola type, she had to admit that the occasional indulgence was decadent. And it was fun to watch her roommate dive into the feast. Yaz had an appetite, that was certain. Grace had repeatedly found herself staring across the table, still trying to figure out where she might know her from, so strong was the feeling of familiarity. Or was it simply attraction? It had been so long since she'd had such a thought that she'd almost choked on her orange juice.

Yaz was easy on the eyes, and handsome enough that likely hers weren't the first to linger. Fortunately, the breakfast feast had also proved a good distraction from another elephant in the room: what were their plans for rhubarb? Talk was kept small. Where they lived. Where they cooked. Where they went to school.

"You did get your list in, didn't you Grace?" Kaley was bouncing in her seat.

In fact, Grace hadn't. She'd gone meticulously through the "provided items" list, and aside from today's ingredient, she'd found every possible ingredient she'd need for her planned dish. Out of consideration, she'd mentioned it to Tiff so that she wouldn't think it was an unintentional omission.

"I can't imagine she didn't," Christian said, loud enough for half the bus to hear. "I've seen her play tennis and she's more competitive than she might appear." He looked around the bus for support. None came. In fact, to Grace's relief, the reaction was a mix of disbelief, annoyance, and couldn't-care-less.

"We might be on a bus, Brassard, but this isn't kindergarten." Yaz's comment was sharp. "Let's face it, we're all competitive. I want to win as much as she does."

Grace appreciated the support and sent a nod of thanks across the aisle.

"God help the person who gets between me and a new fryer for my truck," Rico declared. "Chiles Rellenos don't fry themselves!"

Christian sulked and turned his attention to Vij and Sean, who were talking excitedly about the Canucks win the night before. Grace was leaning over to thank Yaz again for the unexpected defense—though admittedly even she knew how competitive she could be—when Francine turned from several rows ahead to face the group.

"I've only been in Vancouver for a few years, but I can see Mount Baker ahead of us. Shouldn't we be heading to the Okanagan?"

"No need," said Rhonda. "The valley's farms are amazing, true, but the lower mainland is hours closer, and their farms produce even more than the valley. Our restaurant sources almost everything from an organic grower near Mud Bay who's been around since the late 1800s. Crazy to think about, eh?"

"I for one am happy to hear we're staying local," Sean said, rubbing his considerable girth. "Lunch is already too far away. And another protein option would've been nice. I don't consider yogurt as anything other than good milk gone bad."

"No joke. Maybe they'll let us eat our way through the rhubarb patch."

The response to Vij's comment was laughter, but like spoiled milk, Sean's comment sat in Grace's stomach and soured. No one else had eggs benny? She dared not ask out loud. Instead, she looked at Yaz, who sat quietly with brow furrowed. *She'd heard it too.* While breakfast was delicious, being treated differently didn't sit well. Grace's eyes narrowed. She opened her notebook and scribbled a note in large letters: *Call Mr. Barney.*

❖

The scant bit of makeup each contestant had received onboard the bus was just enough to take the sheen off their cheeks. As it was being applied to Grace, Yaz found herself wondering why it was necessary, because was it even possible to make Grace look more radiant? More classically perfect? The woman was flawless. And clearly used to having makeup applied. Yaz had squirmed in her seat, uncomfortable with the entire process. More uncomfortable was the fact that she could feel Grace's eyes on her as the obviously irritated makeup artist held her chin firmly while applying the powder, and when she looked toward her, Grace quickly looked away but not before Yaz caught the slightest smile.

She didn't think so at first, but the boots turned out to be a good call. Stepping off the bus directly into the spring-soaked earth provided the camera crew and contestants with what Yaz was sure would be entertaining television. Sean almost rolled off his feet, which could've proved catastrophic, but managed with a bit of arm-waving to keep himself upright. Four others went down to their knees. Brassard to his butt. Kaley stepped right out of her mud-mired boot and hopped around until Vij heroically rescued her. Only Grace, she'd noticed, descended from the bus with the elegance of a princess. Yaz wouldn't have been surprised if coats had been thrown beneath her feet. And yes, even in rubber boots Grace was stupidly gorgeous.

No coats were thrown, but Grace was helped onto the wagon by no fewer than three of the guys, obviously eager to keep the princess afloat. She accepted the hands with profuse thanks as she made her way to the top of the stack of hay bales. Yaz doubted Grace had ever seen real hay, or been on an actual farm, and though she'd resisted giving credence to what Brassard had said on the rooftop about Grace's pedigree, it was becoming more and more clear that Grace Donahue possessed a comportment that set her apart. Manor house, yes. Farm, no. Acknowledging that, Yaz wondered why Grace had chosen to be a chef. Hospitality, after all, was a service industry. *And don't rich folks have cooks?* From the bit of conversation they'd shared over breakfast, it seemed like Grace's Cordon Bleu training formed the entirety of her experience with food, short of her business. No discussion of waiting tables. Or bussing them. Or spending long hot hours making stocks, or prepping the mise en place. These duties were part of the grind for most starting out in the industry. Early mornings. Late nights. Grunt work. Not that the French cooking school alone wasn't impressive, but it seemed so formal. So sterile.

Don't judge, Tiger.

Yaz checked her criticism. She knew she was lucky. Maybe not in terms of money in the bank. Definitely not. But in terms of culinary inspiration, fortune had followed. Her great-grandfather immigrated from Singapore to Japan before the occupation during WWII and the food traditions had found their way to her through her inspiration, her mom. She'd nurtured Yaz and her dad with a fusion of Asian influences, creating dishes impossible to find even in Vancouver's extensive Chinatown. Yaz was convinced that if her father hadn't been so controlling, her mom would likely have pursued a professional career in the industry. He took so much from her. *But he lost so much more.*

And then there was Sabrina, who had—despite the challenges presented by the ancient soup kitchen equipment—elevated Yaz's technical college-learned skills to what she'd once enthusiastically declared "near Michelin-worthy." Maybe a bit too enthusiastically, but Yaz agreed that she'd worked hard to improve her skill set and loved Sabrina enough to forgive her the overexuberance. Yaz expected that the next few weeks would be difficult. She hadn't missed a single weekly call with her mom since she'd moved back to Tokyo, and aside from Jenni, who was her assigned "emergency contact," no other outside connection was allowed by rules of the contest.

As the wagon moved toward the fields, Yaz found her attention drawn again to the princess on the hay bale. Who was Grace's village? Who other than the blue-ribbon titans of the most prestigious cooking school in the land had lured her from the banquet to the kitchen? King and Queen Donahue?

Check that meanness, Tiger.

They soon came to a stop at the edge of rows and rows of huge bunches of green-leafed, red-stemmed plants, ending Yaz's royal—and petty—musings. The farm owners were on-site, and keen to explain that the early crop had been covered through the harshest months before being fertilized. Organically. *Of course.*

"Fortunately, April was sunny and warm. This field is five years old, about half of its likely lifetime. We harvest," the affable farmer explained, "through to July, then leave it to restore energy. Today, well, today you harvest. Good luck!"

CHAPTER SIX

Round One, Day Three

The bus to the studio the next morning was much quieter. Grace assumed it was because everyone, herself included, was reviewing their notes and sorting out their nerves before the first in-the-studio-kitchen shoot of *Recipe for Success*. Fortunately, everyone had access to an exceptional crop of rhubarb. The ripe vegetable grew plentifully at ground level, and the varieties offered a myriad of possibilities, including stalks that were striped and polka-dotted. Sean had loaded his basket to well above the brim.

"I'm not sure what he's making," Kew joked, "but if he uses everything he harvested, his dish will certainly be rhubarb-forward!"

She'd selected one named for Queen Victoria that had gorgeous rich red in the stalk. Not all the contests' challenges would be as easy, but if this season was like last, the producers would no doubt balance the easy pickings with something much more arduous.

At dinner the previous night, Grace had been invited to sit with Kaley and Francine, two contestants who filled the hotel restaurant with high-energy conversation and laughter. Rhonda and Rico seemed to be getting along well, seated at a table for two and apparently oblivious to any other diners. Christian arrived late and sat at the bar with Tiff, who stayed only long enough to finish her drink before heading off with a takeout box. When he looked over at their table, Grace shrugged as if apologetic that there was no seat for him. She tried not to feel badly for her lack of sincerity; she hadn't missed her parents' extensive circle of friends and was not looking to reconnect with any of them.

Grace had noticed Yaz at a table that included Vij, Sean, and Kew, but she'd appeared more engaged with her notebook than she was with their banter, and by the time Grace had finished her own dinner, Yaz had already left the table. She'd hoped to talk to her about the suite, but her door was closed by the time she got to the room, and anyway, she hadn't been able to connect with the manager, Mr. Barney. So nothing would change soon. With no phone, and being out of the suite all day, today would pose a similar challenge.

The squeal of the limo bus brakes pulled Grace out of her thoughts. They'd arrived at the studio, a large warehouse building with one gigantic exterior wall completely dedicated to an advertisement for *Recipe for Success*. She looked up the bus aisle and saw Yaz looking back in her direction. She was scrunching her hair, and when their eyes met, she looked like she'd been caught with her hand in a cookie jar. She immediately looked up to the left, cracked a crooked smile and threw a two-shoulder *Who, me?* shrug. Grace couldn't resist and smiled back. Yaz was handsome and exactly her type. Type? Didn't that imply plurality of some kind? Could she have a type when there had been just one? If looking counted, then yes. She was definitely looking. Grace shook the debate from her head, gathered her knives and notes, and stepped off the bus behind Yaz, trying hard not to wonder how much more perfectly her khakis could hug her perfect ass. Oh yes, this was going to present an entirely different kind of challenge.

❖

Once inside, the contestants were hustled through a brief round of makeup. Grace watched Yaz squirm against the attention. Grace doubted she had much experience or interest in cosmetics. Frankly, she didn't need it. She had a natural beauty about her. Dark lashes drew attention to her dark brown eyes. Yaz caught her looking and instead of looking away, she set embarrassment aside and allowed herself to linger. It was Yaz who broke their gaze first, but not before Grace elicited a smile.

"Alright, ladies, enough of the mutual admiration society." Tiff leaned through the doorway and tapped her watch. "We're ready for you. Grace, you're up first. Stage Two, on the left. We're just shooting a short bio to introduce you to our viewers. Easy peasy. Yaz, I'll be back for you soon."

Grace walked through the studio, carefully avoiding the tangles of electrical cords and squinting against the incomprehensible numbers of lights that beamed down from banks high above. Tiff followed, directing her to a stool in the center of the room, a space really, surrounded by long black curtains. Cameras, at least three, and probably the same number of microphones suspended from long boom rods, circled her. After a few encouraging words by Tiff and the director, a pink-haired hipster-looking woman named Mickey, Grace took a deep breath and signaled that she was ready.

"I'm Grace Donahue," she began comfortably. "I'm the owner and head chef of Let 'Em Meat Pie, Vancouver's pop-up pie place. I grew up in North Vancouver, and I'm super excited to be here competing against these amazingly skilled chefs and highlighting the bounty of our great province." Finishing school had given her a comfort speaking in front of people, and she was able to imagine that the camera was just that...a group of people who loved food as much as she did.

Once done, Tiff took her through the studio maze and into a room where she joined the rest of the contestants. "Welcome to the Stew 'n' Brew Room, people. Make yourselves comfortable. You'll be spending a good part of your day in here, waiting for calls to set, and thinking about what you will create, or have created, in studio. Hence, stew. We'll start calling you to the set once the rigging, audio, and cameras are all in perfect place. And believe me, that takes time. There's a fridge with beverages of all sorts, hence brew, and some sandwiches. Help yourself, but remember, you'll want your wits about you when you're called to the studio kitchens. We will stagger your start times by ten minutes so that your dishes land on the judges' table while hot."

"I don't get it," Kaley said, a bewildered look on her face.

"We don't want to disadvantage anyone, especially when there are ten of you. If you do the math for the first round, allowing the judges ten minutes to taste and render their decisions, there would be ninety minutes between the first and last adjudication. That's a long time to hold the temperature of a dish. So, we stagger your start times, but you still all get the same amount of time to cook."

"Okay, that sounds fair." Kaley still looked a bit uncertain but seemed to have grasped the concept.

Tiff remained patient and clarified further. "Our viewers don't know it, but our team of post-production editors splice and dice to make it look like everyone arrived at their stations at the same time."

"And we will all be together on set for a period of time, right?" Kaley seemed, at last, enthused.

"Yes. You will. But not in every round. It will depend on the length of the given cooking time."

Tiff didn't look at Kaley to see if she'd sorted out the math. Grace could see that she had. Instead, Tiff continued to explain that once your time was complete, you would present your dish to the judges. "You may be asked questions about your dish. Try to be succinct. We will move very quickly through this process because except for the final contestant, another chef will follow you with their dish. The judges will tell you what they think. Be professional. And respectful. Once everyone has had their dish appraised in detail, you will all return for a summary of the judgments. It's at that point that one of you will be asked to hang up your apron and leave the studio."

A collective gulp filled the room as Tiff left to check on the set readiness. The Stew 'n' Brew Room was perfectly named. As they waited for the first chef to be called, Grace could feel the nervous energy swirling within the four green walls. They spent most of the morning making small talk, studying notes, and clearly aware that the game was afoot. Even Yaz, who appeared self-assured most of the time, was gnawing on her pencil top like a hungry beaver.

When at last Tiff returned, she reminded them that cameras would be rolling when they each entered. She showed them on a map of the studio kitchen exactly where their station would be. Their time would start when they entered, so they were to go directly to their stations and begin to load up in the pantry and prepare their dishes. "Rico, you're number one."

Grace was aware that an eerie silence had descended amid the remaining chefs. Stew was right. She was called in sixth, and the first thing she noticed on entering the expansively lit studio was the immensity of the set. There were ten cooking stations, half already in full swing. Each station was equipped with a full set of professional-grade appliances. The pantry was along the back wall, downstage, while the judges' table was on a dais located upstage left. When she reached her station, Grace placed her knife bag beside her basket of rhubarb and unrolled it. She then turned her attention to the task at hand and headed to the pantry. She was here for one reason. Her business. She'd built Let 'Em Meat Pie and had shielded it from her parents' intrusion. She'd ignored their obvious disapproval when she insisted on going to culinary school instead of using her finance degree for her family's empire. Not that she wasn't grateful for her degree, especially when it came to budgeting for her shop, but soon her parents' displeasure evolved into an insidious undermining of her achievements. The last straw was when her dad bought the property that Let 'Em Meat Pie rented solely to reno-vict her "for your own good." Her debts were mounting, and it would've been easy to give up. She came up with a new plan. She put as much distance from her family as she could. No visits. No contact. Then, she applied to be a contestant on *Recipe for Success*. Her business, her future, was why she was here, and she wasn't going to let it, or herself, down.

The distractions of the lights and the judges and the enormity of the kitchen eventually settled, and she found herself in a good groove. She looked over at Yaz, who'd been called out to set just ahead of her. She was met with a brief smile before Yaz's laser focus was turned back to what looked from the short distance like a duck breast. Grace lingered over the keen attention she was paying to the scoring of the thick fatty skin of the bird. Once seasoned, it was placed in the cast-iron pan where it sizzled and spat its juices, the smoke wafting across the room and filling Grace's nose with warm and herbaceous aromatics. Yaz managed the sear expertly, lifting the duck breast from the pan with tongs only when a golden diamond-shaped crust had formed evenly across the skin. She suspended the breast, patiently waiting until its legendary renderings dripped back into the hot pan. Only then did she flip it over and gently return it to the unctuousness pooled in the cast-iron vessel. Intentional and exacting. Focused. *Like I should be.* Grace glanced at her timer. Was she in some crazy kind of black hole? She must be, because that was the only explanation for how so much time had been swallowed up so quickly. Grace turned her attention to her Bavarian cream and worked with full speed. She had just put the finishing touches on her dish when her buzzer sounded. She let out the breath she'd been holding for what seemed like forever and stepped back from her workstation. Looking around, she realized that five contestants had already left the kitchen for adjudication.

She took a moment to assess her effort, a nicely executed charlotte russe cake filled with rhubarb bavarois and decorated with raspberries and candied rhubarb. It stood elegantly pink at the edge of an impressively clean workstation on a white china pedestal plate. We eat first with our eyes, she recalled hearing once, and the cake certainly looked delicious. She'd once seen a pastry instructor at the Cordon Bleu substitute macarons for the cake's fortress of ladyfingers and adopted the variation to highlight the rhubarb again in the filling for the meringue cookies. Her classic training seemed to have carried her through the nerves. The dish's color and form appeared spot-on. Taste, she hoped, would match. Most importantly, she'd completed the task despite the time warp and within budget. According to plan.

She followed the stagehand's direction to the judges' table, noticing as she passed Yaz's empty station that it looked quite unlike her own. It was as if a bomb had gone off. Smoke from the sear still wafted above the cooktop. Food-splattered linens had been tossed amidst dishes and pans that teetered on top of each other. The last she'd seen, Yaz was deftly multitasking the completion of a sauce, the refinement of what appeared to be an orange peel garnish, and the beginning of plating. Calm amid chaos. Impressive.

Grace almost bumped into the back of the stagehand as he stepped aside past a bank of cameras and indicated a marked x on the studio floor. Once there, she looked toward the dais. Her initial relief and pride ebbed as each adjudicator came into view. She recognized the show's distinguished stars, Eleanor Tremblay, Marcus Perrin, and Carolyn Conceptione. With them today was a guest judge, who she realized with some dread was the notorious but fair celebrity chef, Randi Solari.

Ten minutes after serving them, Grace returned to the Stew 'n' Brew, her poise crumbling like her dessert had. She was not alone. Sean, Rico, Vij, and Kaley also sat quietly, their energy shifted from the pre-cook anticipation to what appeared to be an uncomfortable anxiety as they waited for everyone to return and then head back for the summaries. Only then would they know how their judging compared with the others. No one volunteered to share. And no one asked. Not even Kaley, who was twirling her hair five fingers at a time. Yaz was the only one who seemed impossibly calm and cool. Grace's stomach was in a knot, and time, which had somehow been sped up while cooking, was now measured in ten-minute increments. One by one, the remaining four competitors returned, each of them looking somewhere on a spectrum between shell-shocked and devastated. When Francine returned, she was wiping her eyes and avoided Grace's attempt to console her. Instead, she'd grabbed her coat and signaled to Sean that a smoke was in order. *Another industry pitfall.* As they'd walked out, Grace heard her muttering something about Eleanor Tremblay, part of which was "…everyone I worked with in Montreal said she was a bitch…why is she a judge? What does she know about B.C.?"

Sean responded to Francine supportively, explaining that whatever the judge had said could not possibly have been worse than his critique. "Marcus Perrin said that my fennel and strawberry and rhubarb lamb was 'confused'…what the heavenly jeez is that supposed to mean?"

After an impossibly long and still silent hour, they were all asked to return to the studio. They followed each other, and Grace smiled thinking that they marched like children being called to the principal's office. Under the lights, they were placed in a line in front of the judges. As the brief summaries of the first five contestants were read, Grace's eyes wandered down the line toward Yaz. She stood tall and straight, her eyes bright. She must've done well. *Good.* And she had. The duck, Grace soon learned, was a success, and Yaz's perpetual cool broke with a smile. She only half-heard Kaley's summary because of the dull murmur in her ears, caused by her blood pounding with anxiety, or maybe something else. Yaz's smile was very, very nice. She wanted to linger but felt the lights brighten on her face and realized it was her turn. She crossed her fingers as her own assessment was read.

"Grace, the judges liked your rhubarb charlotte cake though the crumb was a bit off the standard. They loved your star anise rhubarb macaron accents, but overall felt you played it too safe." Much more succinct than the critique she'd received minutes earlier, but equally fair. She owned that a dessert was a bit easy, given that rhubarb, fruit or not, was expected to be paired with sweets. The macaron's spice profile hopefully showed the judges some creativity, but she couldn't help but wonder if she'd done enough to make it through. Playing it safe. Where had she heard *that* before? With so much riding on it, why had she not pushed the envelope? Taken more chances. Because the plan was to stay, and to do that, risk must be mitigated. She didn't want to go.

Her fear was in her throat as the judges completed the last four summaries and announced their decision. In the end, it was Sean who was asked to say good-bye. This was just the first round. Not perfect. But at the very least, Grace thought with great relief and some sadness as she watched Sean leave the studio, it's not my last.

CHAPTER SEVEN

Round One, Day Four

Yaz let herself sleep in. Except for today's short post-cook interviews, where contestants were asked how they felt about the results of the previous day's cooking and judging, it was for the most part a day off. Her interview was scheduled for early afternoon, and it was in the makeshift hotel studio so no need to commute to the main stage. She was exhausted from the previous day's events. Yes, they'd only had ninety minutes to cook, but it was beyond stressful and left her spent.

Grace had been out of sorts since the judges' reviews. Her exuberant demeanor had taken a back seat to an intensity Yaz suspected had something to do with the critique of her dish. Not wanting to be presumptuous, she'd invited her to watch a bit of mindless television rather than query the source of her angst. Grace had only lasted through one episode of *House of Dragons* before heading off to bed. This morning, she'd gone out without touching breakfast.

Yaz had secretly hoped for another morning of her company over the usual fare, eggs benny. Well, specifically more of the hollandaise sauce because anyone can poach an egg, right? *Best mother sauce ever.* The hotel's creamy buttery blanket hadn't been the expected industrially-packaged affair. Its consistency had been diabolically perfect, and she was picking up on something beyond the tarragon, a sweetness of sorts. Nutmeg? No. Cinnamon. Really, Yaz? Cinnamon? What was it about cinnamon lately? She couldn't shake it from her nostrils. She'd hoped that day three of the decadent eggs would give her a chance to identify the sauce's subtle undertones—provided her arteries survived the quest—but when she lifted the metal cloche, two enormous Belgian waffles stared back at her. She dug in, her hollandaise pursuit put on mental hold. She wanted to feel badly that the other competitors were chewing on granola, but the waffles made that impossible. *As waffles are wont to do.*

As she indulged, she wondered if maybe Grace was still upset about the preferential breakfasts they'd been receiving, and not eating was her way of protesting. That would be virtuous, but sad because, damn, these waffles were crazy good! More likely Grace's somber mood was due to the feedback she'd received on her rhubarb dish. Criticism about one's food was hard not to take personally, and even with a good review, Yaz had felt surprisingly vulnerable in front of the panel. After all, these were expert chefs and restauranteurs. And she was a line cook. The hierarchy was legit. It took years back of house to achieve executive status.

The couch called to her after breakfast, and she curled under the throws and reflected on her first round. She'd presented the judges with a cardamom-crusted duck breast with roasted rhubarb and a mandarin gastrique.

"Why mandarins?" Marcus Perrin had asked. "It's an unusual pairing with rhubarb, but somehow the addition of cardamom makes it work."

Yaz explained that mandarins were a main export from Japan to B.C., and a tradition of reciprocity since the late 1800s. "And the cardamom is a core part of many Japanese curries. I wanted to honor both legacies in my dish and hoped that the two flavors would make sense."

"I think you've achieved that. One concern, though. You roasted the rhubarb, which intensifies its flavor, especially against the strong protein. But it also gives the dish sweetness. Maybe too much?" said Chef Perrin. *That's fair.*

"I agree," added Chef Solari, "but when eaten as a whole, the dish is saved by the orange and rhubarb gastrique which is delicious and lends acidity to balance the rhubarb with the richness of the duck."

"I would say that the dish is strong, but it does come perilously close to the budget restriction," said Carolyn Conceptione, who had put her fork down and was reviewing the tablet that each contestant submitted to the panel with their dish to show the food costs for the dish. Yaz remembered that at this point her mouth became pasty and dry. She'd had no previous experience with costing, except what she'd learned in her college courses. Line cooks were seldom expected to manage that aspect of the business. She knew it showed in what she'd submitted.

All in all, though, with rhubarb now in the rearview mirror, she was prepared to take the good with the bad. She had Sabrina to thank for that too. She'd cautioned Yaz that the judges were going to be critical, but ultimately, they were human. And sometimes humans were fallible. Who would know better than Sabrina Marline? "The spotlight had been too bright," she'd once said when Yaz asked how she ended on the periphery of the industry. "The business burned me." *It, and the whiskey.* Sober for four years, though, the once-lauded chef had landed at the shelter, and seemed content to help feed Vancouver's unhoused, abused, and otherwise vulnerable populations. Addiction was a familiar path for Yaz, having walked it with her addict father for years, so as fallible as Sabrina may have become through one lens, Yaz saw her through another and heeded her advice. "The important thing is to take what you are hearing and decide what sits right in your gut."

Yaz had survived this round. And so had others. She hoped Grace could listen to her own inner voice and not take the judges entirely to heart. After all, she surely hadn't created a successful business without a certain amount of fortitude. *And likely a bit of Donahue cash.*

❖

Yaz was showered and dressed by eleven and decided to go for a walk around the hotel property before her interview. As she passed the hotel lobby bar, she was hailed by Kaley to join her, Kew, and Christian for a coffee. She liked Kaley and Kew enough so decided that she could tolerate Brassard for the length of time it took to enjoy an oat milk flat white.

"Can you believe how quickly time flew by?" Kaley shook her head, "I almost cried when my timer hit the one-minute mark!"

"And at least half the cook time was spent going from work surface to appliances...I have never been in a kitchen that big!" Kew turned to Yaz. "You had a great dish. I would've loved to have tasted it."

"Well, I would've stood in line for hours to taste that grilled halibut with, what was it? A Szechuan pepper-compressed rhubarb?" Yaz asked.

"Kew, it was really impressive," Kaley raved.

After just one round, Yaz felt sure that Kew would stay in the competition for a few more rounds. The fact that he worked at one of Vancouver's trendiest haute cuisine establishments showed in his dish.

"Thanks. I'm sad to see Sean go, though. He was a fun guy. And a fellow Canucks fan."

"I still think Calgary's Flames are going to take them down though. They usually crumble in the playoffs."

"Really, Christian? You're not cheering for the home team?" Yaz was not surprised by his treasonous suggestion but enjoyed poking the little bear.

"I haven't been a fan since they added those two foreign guys to their roster." His comment was met with silence. *Talk about not reading the room.* He pivoted quickly, an ability Yaz guessed had come with plenty of practice. "I still think Francine should've gone home first. Her dish was a mess." *Plenty of practice.*

At least Francine's dish was creative. Brassard had cooked a dish that even the judges noted was "safe," a brie and green peppercorn crostini with rhubarb compote. But it was within budget and the judges agreed it was well executed. At least enough to get by.

Brassard continued to fill the silence. "Sean only lost because he made it complicated. Keep it simple, stupid, that's my motto."

You got stupid right.

To Kew and Kaley's credit, neither joined in his disparaging rant and they found reasons to leave Brassard to finish his iced frappa-whatever on his own. Joining the exodus, Yaz wondered if backstabbing was common in all professions. She'd already had to sidestep other objectionable behaviors in her short career. She'd even left an apprenticeship at a restaurant with a solid reputation but an unsavory executive chef. This competition, though, was another opportunity that would never come up again and she wanted, no needed, to keep her wits about her and avoid being sucked down by the likes of Brassard.

❖

Yaz took the stairs up to the mezzanine level and headed toward the sports complex, a dome connected to the hotel by a short catwalk. Through the bank of windows that lined the far side of the entrance, she could see a vast array of lights suspended beneath a white fabric ceiling. As she approached, several tennis courts dotted with high visibility yellow balls came into view. She could see a machine firing balls toward someone below, and an equal number, with similar velocity, flying back toward it. Most hit within the court's white lines. It was only as she moved closer to the window that she could see who was responsible for the returns.

Grace.

She wore a tailored white tennis skirt with a pink sleeveless polo. She was facing the machine, in the classic receive-ready pose, waiting for each ball, anticipating its speed and direction, and quickly shifting accordingly to make the return volley. Yaz admired her proficiency. Such coordination. And anger. Grace was hammering the balls as though they'd stolen her allowance, each stroke showcasing her shapely, muscled shoulders. These angled down to Yaz's second favorite spot on a woman, the mesmerizingly soft slope below the ear. Each follow-through of Grace's stroke was made more forceful by athletic legs. Long legs. Nice legs. Really nice…

"Hey there."

A voice that sounded strangely familiar interrupted her daydream and her cheeks flushed.

"Sorry, didn't mean to startle you."

Yaz turned to face the woman whose voice she was still trying to place.

"Hi, uh…"

"I'm Lyn. Lyn Sanyal. You're Yaz, right?"

"Right." It struck her then. *Gracie.* From the suite that first day. The raspy voice. This was who Grace had been talking to. "Yes, sorry, I am Yaz. Sano. You're Bette's wife, right? I saw you with her on the rooftop during the reception. And you know Grace?"

"Hi, Yaz. Nice to meet you. Yes, I'm Bette's better half, though she'd probably contest that!" Lyn laughed as she shook Yaz's hand. "And yes, I know Grace."

Yaz didn't want to assume how and was pleased that Lyn filled in the blank.

"Joss, my daughter, and she are…were…friends."

Again, as much as Yaz knew there must be a story there, and as curious as she was to hear it, she held her tongue and looked back down at Grace, who continued smashing yellow balls back at the machine. Her blond hair was tucked into the back of the cap she wore, but with each violent impact, it strayed, forcing Grace to tuck it back under the cap or behind her ears every few volleys.

"I read in your bio that you volunteer at the Harbor Shelter…you must know Sabrina Marline. How is she?"

Yaz detected a friendliness in Lyn's question, but she was guarded when it came to what she would reveal about her mentor. "She's good."

Lyn must've picked up on her tentativeness because she went on to explain how she was aware of the challenges Sabrina had faced over the years. "It's a hard business. More so even now for women. The culture that once kept us out is now letting us in, and that includes exposure to the darker side. The after-hours side."

"True."

What she hadn't experienced personally, she'd been filled in on by Sabrina. "How do you come down after ten hours of the most intense and grueling and yes, exhilarating dinner service?" she'd once explained. "Sex. Alcohol. Drugs. Depression. Overly developed egos. A combination of each or the whole shooting match for some."

"I'm glad that Grace has her own shop," Lyn said. "It keeps her out of harm's way, though if she learned anything from her family, it's how to maintain a single focus. Once that girl has a notion to do something, she does it."

"She hasn't talked a lot about her family."

"That doesn't surprise me. They are formidable." Lyn looked around the room. "I'm surprised they don't own this place yet."

"This place? Like, this hotel?"

"This hotel. It's rare to find a hotel in Vancouver that the Donahue empire doesn't have its fingers in. It's lucky that Bette was able to find this one—neutral ground, so to speak— or you and the rest of the crew would be commuting to B.C. from New Zealand."

Pieces were slowly fitting into place. The penthouse. The luxury breakfasts. What didn't fit was why Grace seemed troubled by the benevolence of her illustrious clan.

"Why is she so mad?" she asked as Grace incessantly and ruthlessly hammered the balls. "She didn't get cut, and she wasn't even in the bottom two."

Lyn laughed out loud. "Grace is very hard on herself. Always has been. She'll be fine once she knocks the fuzz off every ball."

Yaz had many more questions she wanted to ask, but she noticed the clock on the wall and realized her interview was imminent. She excused herself and headed down to the meeting room studio. As she did, her thoughts went to the pieces she'd learned about Grace and decided if the picture came together the way she thought, it would be folly to take her own eye off the ball because Grace certainly wouldn't.

Yaz had been back on the suite's sweet couch only a short time when Grace returned. She heard the loud thump of what she imagined was tennis gear being dropped on the tile, then footsteps going into the kitchen. Grace's back was to her so Yaz waited and watched as she poured a glass of water, downed the whole thing, then refilled her glass. It looked as though the storm cloud that had been hanging over the Disney princess's head had somewhat dissipated.

"Looks like someone worked it out this morning! Feeling better?"

Grace spun and leaned against the counter, surprised, then obviously relieved that Yaz wasn't an intruder.

"A bit." Grace took another gulp of water and searched Yaz's eyes over the rim of the glass. "I'm sorry. I know I've been a bit grumpy. I'm also sorry because I need to say again that staying in this suite isn't sustainable. I have a scheduled call with the hotel manager, and I'm going to ask for a different room."

"I get it." Yaz hated to agree, because hey, couch. But she saw how inequity played out at the shelter and knew that getting back on even ground was only fair. "Doesn't mean I won't miss it."

Grace's appreciative smile said it all. And Yaz was all ears.

The sound of the phone ringing put Grace in a sprint to her bedroom, and because the door was left open, Yaz couldn't help but hear one side of the conversation.

"Hello, Mr. Barney. Yes, thank you for responding to my messages."

Pause

"Yes, I understand that this is the Cherry Blossom Festival. I imagine that makes things more difficult. But surely you have one room?"

Pause

"Mr. Barney, you understand that treating me to this lovely suite will in no way serve in your relationship with my father, right? He and I are not exactly on speaking terms, so it may be that you're wasting the lovely gesture on me?"

Pause

"Yes, parents can indeed be that way. Yes, I can understand how you believe that his intentions are good. Still..."

Pause

"I appreciate that, Mr. Barney. When you're speaking with *him*, you can let him know that this intrusion is unwelcome. I'm sure he'll understand."

Pause.

"Yes. Word for word. I appreciate that, Mr. Barney. I'll look forward to hearing from you should a cancelation occur."

Throughout the conversation, Grace remained composed. Crystal clear. Sweet, even. But Yaz could tell she was biting back some tennis-ball-smashing rage, and she was sure that Mr. Barney had detected it too. She thought about what Lyn had said earlier about Grace's single focus. Indeed, there was more to the princess than met the eye. Even more reason to stay focused.

CHAPTER EIGHT

Round Two, Day Two

"Poor Kaley! I hope she recovers."

"I'm sure she will, but I've never seen someone turn green like that. I thought it only happened in cartoons."

Yaz took her usual spot on the couch and Grace fell into the cushions at the other end. They just returned from Round Two's "wonderful adventure in food procurement." Tiff's words, not hers. *Not ever.*

"I am beat," Yaz admitted.

"Same. As if hauling crab traps all morning on the beach wasn't enough, did the producers really need to set us out on a choppy sea on a prawn trawler?"

"I have never been so happy to step back onto solid ground, but I imagine Kaley is."

Grace sighed. "It was beautiful out there, though. Seeing Pacific Rim National Park from the water? Stunning." She was familiar with the Strait of Georgia, the large body of water separating the B.C. mainland from Vancouver Island. Memories of days aboard her family's sailboat and their weekend retreat on Galiano Island lingered, despite her inclination to scrub the overindulgent opulence she'd been privy to as a youngster from her adult mind. One day she hoped to be better able to filter her past, aware that surely not all those experiences were tainted by the present.

"Yeah, but if I don't see another orange buoy bobbing in synch with my stomach, it'll be none too soon. I'd rather hunt for my shrimp at the Spot Prawn Festival."

"Agreed." She loved the annual spring event held down at False Creek, and she was again transported to memories of her childhood. The Donahues would dock their boat at the nearby club and spend the day walking and eating the delicate shrimp cooked in an unlimited number of ways. Steamed. Spicy. Fried. Raw. Spicy and Raw. Grace felt goose bumps and a strange sensation of someone watching her. She turned and smiled at Yaz, whose lower lip was pinned at the corner between her teeth. It reminded Grace of the first time she saw her from across the table in the very first production meeting. She'd since learned it was a habit that revealed itself whenever Yaz was focused, nervous, or intense. It was endearing. "You're staring."

"Oh, I, uh…sorry, you, er…"

It felt to Grace like the distance between them on the couch had become magnetic, electrified. Weird. Yaz shifted, squirmed, and took firm hold of the arm of the couch at her end, then tried to look casual as she placed a cushion against her thigh between them. Grace looked at the cushion and did all she could to suppress a smile. She wanted to know where Yaz was going with her explanation, and it wouldn't serve to embarrass her further. Poor woman was already red to the tips of her ears. She nodded to encourage Yaz to carry on, enjoying the telltale signs of evasion. Eye contact diminished. Fidgeting increased. Finally, as if she'd landed on the most plausible response, Yaz looked directly at her.

"Sorry. You remind me of someone I used to date. I mean, er…she was, um, also a blonde."

Grace appreciated the display so much she threw out a lifeline. "Did you know that spot prawns are a sustainable harvest?" Change of subject. Classic.

Yaz regained composure with similar speed, the relief obvious on her face. "I hope so because I probably netted ten pounds of the little spotted critters. And they'll have to carry my dish because I only managed to pot two crabs."

"That's sixteen legs and four claws, Yaz," she laughed. "I think you can make it work!"

"Maybe if the room stopped rolling, I'd feel more confident. At least I'm nowhere near as punky as Kaley."

"I'm sure you'll be fine by tomorrow. Let me get you a ginger ale. It'll help settle your stomach."

As Grace stepped up to the kitchenette, she found herself hoping that Yaz's attention was back on her, and she swung her hips just that little bit extra just in case. What the what? Was she flirting? Was Yaz? What was going on? *Nothing, Grace, it's your imagination.* Or wasn't it? *She's your roomie. Whatever it is or isn't, it's not going to happen.* There was too much at stake. She pulled a can of soda from the well-stocked fridge and was reminded of her conversation with the hotel manager. "I'm sorry again about not being able to get us a different room. Mr. Barney said he'd let us know if something opened up." Another classic subject change.

"No need to apologize." Yaz slowly brought herself upright and grabbed the TV remote. "It's cherry blossom time. The hotel is probably full up. Do you mind if I put on some music?"

"God, no! I miss it. It's amazing how many things we rely on our phones for, right?"

"At least they gave us access to SiriusXM. Oh, I love this song." Yaz turned up the volume and moved in rhythm to the sound.

"So Jealous? Oh, I like this remix. Always an acoustic girl, personally."

"Oh, you know Tegan and Sara?"

"Not personally, but I've been a fan since I was a teenager." Grace noted a look of surprise on Yaz's face. "Yes, I am that old."

Yaz laughed. "Me too. The Beaches are my fave at the moment." She stopped couch-dancing, leaned back, and patted her stomach. "I can't believe I'm saying this, but I'm grateful the big breakfasts have stopped. I can't imagine how we'd have felt on that boat with a belly full of waffles."

Grace opened the can and handed it to Yaz. "Heard. And that's saying a lot because I know you love your waffles."

"And benny. But no worries, I still feel pretty spoiled."

Grace watched as Yaz brushed her hand along the couch cushion. "It's all about that couch, isn't it?"

"Mmmm. So niiice…"

Grace laughed and took a seat next to her. She was right about the couch.

"In case you're wondering, it turns out that as suspected, my dad was the puppet master of this whole room debacle. He, well, he is…" She had many choices of words to describe her father. *Intrusive. Persistent. Smothering.* But there was no need to explore that broken branch of the family tree with Yaz. She did, for some reason she hadn't quite landed on yet, want Yaz to know her better, and her family continued to be an unpleasant yet unavoidable part of her story. "He has some issues with entitlement." Good, enough said. "My grannie, not his mom, but my mom's mom, was my real hero."

"How so?" Yaz asked, continuing to stroke the couch as if it were a family pet.

"She's why I went to the Cordon Bleu. In fact, she's also how I went to the Cordon Bleu." By the look on Yaz's face, Grace knew she needed to elaborate. First, she needed to swallow back the emotions that always came up when she thought about her favorite grandparent. She took a sip of her bubbly water, then looked to see that Yaz was still intent on an explanation. Her eyes were intently focused, so Grace took a breath and began. "My grannie was amazing. She owned a diner in Kitsilano, not far from the museum. She and my grandpa Joe, who died before I was born, built the restaurant themselves. Grannie Jean cooked, and he ran the business end."

Yaz sat up as if electrocuted. "Wait. Grannie *Jean*? As in Jean and Joe's?"

Grace laughed. "Yes, that's the place. You know it?"

"It's a Vancouver institution. *The* Jean and Joe's, in Kits?" Yaz blinked as if she couldn't believe what she was hearing.

Grace shouldn't have been surprised. The diner was a landmark for almost a half century in the trendy Kitsilano neighborhood. Any place with that kind of longevity would have a far-reaching reputation. "It was, yes."

"I'm sorry, I didn't know they'd closed down." Yaz seemed genuinely sad. "Their waffles, to this day I swear, none compare. This hotel's included."

"They were the best, right?"

"Sorry, I took you off course there. Waffles do that to me. So, you were saying about your grannie…"

"Grannie Jean passed away, actually, a year after I finished university." Grace paused to accept Yaz's nod of condolence, then went on to explain that she, along with all her cousins, received a small inheritance. "It was enough to give me some choices I didn't have before."

"The Cordon Bleu?"

"Yes. That was the easy choice. I'd waited tables at the diner and spent enough time in the kitchen to know I preferred both to sitting behind a desk running numbers for some faceless corporation."

"I'm not sure I understand what other choices you mean."

Grace could see that Yaz was perplexed about something additional but would ask about it later. For now, back to the broken family tree branch. What could she share that didn't hint at the disconnect she felt when she thought about her parents, let alone talk about them? Grace knew her hesitation was only increasing Yaz's curiosity, so she jumped in and hoped she could be fair and impassive. "My mom was embarrassed by the diner. As she is by any service industry, really. I'm not sure how she came to that belief, given how Grannie Jean and Grandpa Joe provided for her in every way possible, but she was uncomfortable with being the kid whose parents owned the diner, regardless of how important it was to the community, or how appreciated and respected her parents were. She was further mortified that I worked there because by then, she'd climbed the social ladder and couldn't possibly explain to the 'ladies who lunch' why her university graduate daughter was not working for the Donahue empire."

"Oh, jeez, Grace. That sounds awful."

"It was. The choice that was most difficult was what to do with the remainder of the inheritance. I wanted to pay my parents back for my education, hoping it would release me somehow. But I didn't have enough to do it and if I still owed them even a penny, they'd lord it over me. Probably double the interest." Grace tried to smile so that Yaz would think she was joking, but the truth was that she believed the possibility existed.

"So what did you do?"

"I doubled down. Knowing I couldn't have their approval unless I followed their rules, I took the balance and used it to start Let 'Em Meat Pie when I came back from the Cordon Bleu. I'm still in building mode, so the revenue isn't quite there yet. But hopefully it will be, and until then, I just try to keep the wolves from the gate, so to speak."

"That explains why this room, including this impossible-to-replicate couch, is especially problematic." It looked as though Yaz had started to appreciate the cost to Grace. "It comes with a price tag that has your name on it."

"Yes, it does." She was sweet, and Grace appreciated that she was trying to ease the tension that must've registered on her face. She was just about to apologize for monopolizing the conversation when she noticed a flesh tone adhesive bandage sticking out from Yaz's sleeve.

"What is that?" Grace realized she sounded alarmed, but as she looked closer it was obvious that the injury required more than a bandage. The area around the base of Yaz's thumb was red and swollen. She attempted to pull her sleeve back down over it, but Grace gently grabbed hold of her wrist and pulled herself closer. "How did this happen?"

"It's nothing, really. I kinda burned it a bit when I lost my grip on the shrimp net line. Just missed pinching my hand in the puller block."

"*Burned it a bit?*" Grace peeled back the bandage carefully and pushed up Yaz's sleeve, revealing a stunning tiger-striped tail and a blistering wound. The portion of the tattoo she could see was beautiful and intriguing, but right now there were more important things to deal with. "Yaz, this could get infected. I've got something for it. Hang on."

Grace hurried to her bedroom and riffled through her gym bag looking for her small first aid kit. She was always getting blisters and hoped she hadn't used all the tape and gauze. *Got it. Perfect.* On her way back to the living room, she stopped in the kitchen, filled a bowl with cold water and took the roll of paper towels off the holder, tucking it under her arm. Grace sat thigh to thigh with Yaz on the couch and motioned for her to show her hand. Her patient was no longer resisting and turned her palm up. A small straight line the same width as the shrimp gear's rope had marked its way from the bottom of Yaz's palm to just above her wrist.

She wet the tip of a piece of towel and gently dabbed it on the wound. Once satisfied it was clean, Grace smoothed a bit of ointment on it as gently as she could. She could feel the heat radiating from the sore. She then placed a piece of gauze over the worst spots, wrapped a bit more around the wrist and thumb, and applied a few pieces of medical tape to hold her efforts in place.

When the dressing was done, she realized that she hadn't let go of Yaz's hand. The fingers she held were long and almost masculine, the palm wide and slightly calloused where the bandage didn't cover. A working hand. She realized her own thumb was slowly caressing the lower pads of Yaz's fingers. Yaz was so still Grace wondered if she was breathing. As if doing them both a favor, she took a deep breath and released the bandaged hand, placing hers gently on Yaz's thigh. She felt a wetness begin to build where her own thighs met. She shifted and silently cursed her reaction. *Nope. Not going to happen.*

"So tell me more about the shelter," she said, withdrawing her hand and gathering up her first aid items, all while wondering how she'd never noticed Yaz's long, dark eyelashes.

"Ah, yes. The shelter. So, I first came across it a few years ago. I was looking for my dad."

Grace listened as Yaz shared with her what she could only describe as a tragedy.

"He'd entered into a bad deal that cost him his importing business. And most of what we owned. I was around sixteen at the time. He was so filled with shame and instead of leaning on my mom and I, he retreated. Started with drinking. That lasted about a year before he turned to street drugs. At that point, he'd left us. I guess he couldn't bear for us to see him. Didn't want to bring his shame home. I knew that he was living on East Hastings somewhere, and that's where I went looking. Never found him but eventually the police did. Couldn't revive him. Fentanyl."

Yaz had recited the story with little emotion, as if it was a set of historical facts she'd recounted time and time again. But when she was done, a small quiver of her chin revealed the pain. Grace placed her hand back on Yaz's thigh.

Yaz stepped out the melancholy. "It's okay. I'm okay now. It was back then I found the shelter. And met Sabrina."

She could tell that the emotions had been too close for Yaz's comfort, and she went along with the redirection. "It's nice that you have Sabrina—and of course your mom and Jenni—looking out for you."

Yaz covered Grace's hand with her own.

"It's not for me to say, but your dad, Grace? Maybe he's trying in the only way he knows how. I'm sure he cares, right? I mean, he's gone out of his way to pamper you…" Yaz looked around the suite, "…and lucky me."

Grace appreciated that Yaz might think her dad's motives were good. *I'm sure even he thinks so.* She shook her head. "With my dad, it's always business. He's trying to close a deal with this hotel and is simply trying to ingratiate himself with its owners. The room. The meals. They're part of the game. He doesn't care about me, or fair play, as much as he cares about his winning reputation."

Funny, Grace thought as she heard the words come out of her mouth. Winning was also her goal. But she wasn't using her family to do it. In fact, she didn't want anything to do with her overbearing family at all. *Recipe for Success* was her way out from under them.

She realized Yaz was asleep when Yaz's hand slid off hers. Rather than wake her, she quietly moved off the couch and lifted Yaz's legs, swiveling and repositioning her to make her more comfortable. It was early, but tomorrow was Round Two's cooking day and Tiff had explained that not just one, but two contestants would be going home in a "double elimination." Grace planned to be around for Round Three and as she laid the blanket from the back of the couch over Yaz's sleeping form, she found herself hoping that Yaz would be too.

CHAPTER NINE

Round Two, Day Three

Yaz was relieved to finally be out of the Stew 'n' Brew and on her way to the set. Her start time was mid-group, and the wait was agonizing. Nervousness churned, though at least this time she had an idea of what to expect. She knew from the first round where equipment was, how the pantry was organized, and what it felt like to be working under the bright lights of the studio kitchen. She was also clear in her mind the approach needed to create her dish in the allotted time. She'd budgeted time for added touches, knowing that her methodology seemed a bit different from the other contestants; less methodology, if she were honest, and a bit more seat-of-her-pants, go-with-the-flow given the ingredients sort of approach. But nonetheless, she felt focused as she at last made her way onto set.

Focused. For at least two minutes.

Until she noticed Grace, whose start time was thirty minutes ahead of hers. And that thirty minutes was time enough to demonstrate a noticeable shift in her methodology. Grace's station, which last round was an almost unimaginably pristine bastion of orderliness, had been flipped on its head. Grace too. Her hair had escaped its tie-back, falling into her eyes and across her shoulders, the whole wavy blond mess of it bouncing as Grace paced back and forth with atypical aimlessness between the blast chiller and her station. She gazed at the timer every three seconds, it seemed, waiting, apparently, for something. What, exactly, Yaz could not tell. She calculated quickly in her mind that Grace probably had thirty or so minutes left, but it wasn't clear yet what stage her dish was at, let alone what it was. Odd. Scrambling Grace was not what she'd expected to see. Where was neat as a pin, ultra-organized in-the-kitchen Grace? This Grace was more consistent with in-the-suite Grace, the woman whose clothes, shoes, and racquet quite literally lay wherever they landed. Also odd. Maybe round two Grace was the real Grace, and round one was an exception? Odder yet was how much Yaz had noticed. Feck. *Focus, girl.*

Yaz opened up her knife bag and laid out her instruments, The crab and shrimp she'd caught yesterday was in a cool bin, and she set immediately to cleaning it. These were familiar ingredients, as the menu at Lola's included three shellfish dishes plus a seasonal special. Within minutes, shells were piled high and she could turn her attention to gathering items needed from the pantry.

That's where she ran into Grace. Messy Grace, who bounced along the dry ingredient shelves, shifting items with frenetic determination.

"Can I help you find something?"

Grace turned and Yaz immediately saw the tears begin to fill the baby blues.

"I can't," she choked, "I can't find the agar-agar. I swear it was here, and it's on the list, but I can't find it."

Yaz's heart was stricken. "Grace, tell me what your dish is." She kept her voice low and calm, hoping it would ebb Grace's tidal panic. "Maybe I can help."

"It was supposed to be a sweet pea and prawn panna cotta with crab mousseline. I was forced to use gelatin because I couldn't find the agar-agar. It hasn't set."

Yaz looked at the clock, its red neon numbers telling her that little could be done to salvage a stubborn panna cotta. Her mind churned, flipping through cookbooks she'd read, thinking about her lessons with Sabrina. Do she really have time for this? It was a competition. *You need to work on your own dish.* Then she looked into those damn eyes. The panic and desperation she saw there was palpable. Damn. No one said you couldn't help another contestant. And this was Grace. Messy, but still Grace. Double damn.

"Pivot."

"Pivot? In less than thirty minutes? Yaz, I didn't budget enough time to—I don't have time to start from scratch,"

"No, you don't. So turn what you've started into something else."

Grace now looked less panicked but more perplexed. She tucked the run-amok hair behind her ridiculously cute ears. "I don't know how I can save…"

Yaz raised her hand in front of Grace as a gesture for her to stop spinning and waited until she had her attention. She quickly scanned the pantry. The camera operator was at the other end of the room, filming Kaley as she picked through the fresh herb section. There was nothing wrong with helping a competitor, but Yaz felt as though discretion was warranted. Maybe protecting Grace's ego would add to her own karmic tally. Or maybe it was okay to be nice for no other reason. She leaned in and spoke quietly.

"Île flottante."

"What?"

A bit louder this time. "Île flottante. The ingredients are virtually identical, and I'm sure you could tweak the panna cotta pretty easily. And quickly."

Grace's eyes widened and, like in the movie with the genius mathematician who configured imaginary numbers and formulas that floated in the air, she visibly settled into a new mindset. A beautiful mindset. Her face softened with realization. Hope maybe? She blinked away the tears and grabbed Yaz's arm.

"I could incorporate the mousseline. Oh, and the cloud..." She smiled and her eyes sparkled. "Yes, yes, Yaz. Oh God, you're right. Thank y—"

"Nineteen minutes, Grace. Tick tock." Yaz pulled her arm back, noticing that it instantly tingled as it had last night on the couch. *No time for that.*

"I'm on it." Just like that, confident focused Grace was back. In front of her. Close.

Maybe it was the heat of the battle. Maybe it was the tingling that seemed to be migrating through her body. Or a karmic reward made sexy. But for a second that was surely just split but seemed like infinity-ever-after, Yaz believed that Grace was about to kiss her. She saw Grace's quick look at her lips, she caught the tiny smile, and felt the heat radiating between them as the distance closed. Really? In the pantry? With the camera right there? Like, *right* there. Beside them. Like, *right beside them*. How did that happen?

Grace noticed the camera too, took a deep breath, turned aside, then calmly but quickly moved through the pantry, picking up a few items and heading back to her station.

So no kiss. No karma. Get back to work, Yaz.

❖

How was it possible to resist Grace Donahue?

"Okay, Grace, I'm right behind you." *Not like that.*

Yaz followed her from the limo bus to the hotel's lobby bar, where most contestants landed after a cooking round. Kaley pulled out a chair and waved at them to join her. Normally, Yaz would have passed, but Grace insisted.

"How else can I possibly thank you for what you did today?"

Yaz instantly thought about how she felt on the couch when Grace's fingers had played a symphony on the palm of her hand. And today in the pantry, kisses interruptus. Of course Grace hadn't intended to cause the firestorm that had raged through Yaz's body, a flare-up that had taken every bit of self-control to hose down. She was just being thankful. Kind. Being Grace. But it felt like more, somehow. It had stirred up feelings she hadn't experienced for a long time. She should be the one thanking Grace on behalf of her libido but, well, that was a whole new kind of craziness. And if she thought beyond these wild imaginings that those gut-tightening warm and tingly feelings might be reciprocated? As if. Nonetheless, Yaz needed to work on her discretion. To be caught staring as she was last night, and then mindlessly babble about "someone I used to date," as if there were hordes of discarded blond women devastated in Yaz's wake, was an epic embarrassment. Could she not have come up with a less ridiculous excuse for ogling Grace? Like, maybe she reminded her of Scarlett Johansson? Or Alica Schmidt? But an ex? No. Yaz had never dated anyone with the exquisite but casual beauty of Grace Donahue.

"How does it feel to be a hero, Yaz?" Kew thumped her on the back, disengaging Yaz's mental babble as if it was a hot dog in a windpipe, Heimlich-style, and set a tray with a jug of beer and four glasses on the table.

"Yes." Kaley lifted a beer toward her. "You were epic, Yaz. Grace's hero for sure!"

Yaz wasn't completely surprised that Grace hadn't hesitated to share what had happened, but the fact that she'd spelled out every detail of her plight and spoke about Yaz as if she'd pulled her from a burning building was a bit much. And no mention of the near kiss, which was of course fine because, well, wishful thinking. Other thinking was going on too. Why did she help her? It would've been easy to walk away. To ignore the obvious signs of distress. To be a hard-core competitor. But in addition to the goose-bump-inciting lust that had taken up residence in Yaz's body, there was also contrition. Yep. She'd been wrong. Wrong about Grace being a living put-on-a-pedestal princess. She'd misjudged her. What was it Jenni said about judging? Oh, yeah. *Don't.* Grace hadn't been sent off to the Cordon Bleu with a set of knives and a silver spoon. She'd actually worked in an honest-to-goodness diner. Serving. Bussing. Tiny frilly diner apron. Long blond hair pulled back in a messy ponytail. Soft silky neck exposed. And just like that, regret turned to lasciviousness and Yaz was right back in the goose bump zone. Until Kaley nudged her under the table.

"I hardly think hero status is warranted," she replied, editing herself carefully because Grace's earlier question, *how can I possibly thank you?* was being tossed like a salad through her mind. Spelling out for Grace what thanking her could look like made her smile. *Because that would look like naked.*

Brassard grabbed a chair from the table next to the group and wedged himself in. "What's this about a hero?" he asked, helping himself to a glass. Yaz wasn't surprised he hadn't heard the conversation amongst everyone else on the bus. He was likely too wrapped up in his own bottom three ranking to consider anyone else's experience.

"Yaz saved Grace's ass today." Vij smacked Brassard's head playfully from behind. "Not that you wouldn't have recovered on your own, Grace, I mean you're a great cook!"

"Thank you, Vij, but you are right. In fact, Yaz did rescue me today. And it was all my fault for putting myself in that position. I could've sworn I'd seen agar-agar on the pantry list. And without it, I had no chance of having that panna cotta set in time. And the clock was ticking."

"Time goes so fast, right?" Kaley jumped in. "So Yaz walks over to Grace in the pantry and whispers something in her ear, and voila, Grace transforms the dish and was saved."

Clearly, Kaley watched too many Hallmark movies. Whispering in her ear was an exaggeration. A nice thought, but still. "Technically, I just suggested it would be doable in the time given to turn the sweet pea and spot prawn panna cotta into an île flottante. Grace was the one who actually did it."

"It was so unique, too!" Kaley said, "I don't think a savory île flottante, or even panna cotta, would have ever crossed my mind."

"And she had the ingenuity to accompany it with a mint meringue cloud. I never would've thought of that." she raised her glass toward Grace.

Grace bowed appreciatively. "Not that I didn't appreciate it, Yaz, but you didn't have to help me."

"I sure wouldn't have," muttered Brassard, emptying the jug into his glass and flagging at the bartender for a refill.

No one expected you would.

"I think it was nice," said Francine, "and when Chef Aruna Singh, the queen of Pacific seafood, uses the word 'exquisite' to describe a dish, well, c'est formidable!"

Incredible indeed.

"It was especially generous of her to say so," Grace said.

Yaz felt it was also especially generous of Francine to be so supportive, given how close she had come to being eliminated. The judges had given her a brutal critique for the second round in a row. But they'd raved over Yaz's crab and avocado escabeche accompanied by a spot prawn crudo drizzled with a lemon chili vinaigrette. She'd worried it might be seen as too simple but was confident it would show off each ingredient to its best. It felt like an honest dish, and she allowed herself to feel pride, And she'd managed to come in below budget. Just.

"Kew, I have to say that I thought your dish sounded divine," Grace remarked.

"Thanks. I just wish I could've created that dish within budget."

"And I wish I hadn't created my dish at all." Francine laughed but you could tell there was truth behind it. "Too bad about Rico and Rhonda, though I suspect they'll find comfort somehow."

"Yeah, I don't think being eliminated fazed either one of them." Kew rolled his eyes. "I saw them having their own private Below Deck moment on the boat."

"Talk about *hooking* up!" Vij laughed at his own joke and was met by groans.

"Thanks, Dad," Brassard said while refilling his own glass.

"I guess you never know where you might find love," said Grace.

And then, the inexplicable happened. Or maybe it didn't. Yaz couldn't quite decide, but Grace's statement was immediately followed by a look. A look at Yaz. Like, right in the eyes.

❖

On her way back to the room, Yaz stopped at the lobby grab 'n' go to pick up a package of the foiled chocolates left daily on her pillow by housekeeping. One a day was hardly enough. And chocolate would have to suffice for the other sweet indulgence that had been on her mind all day. Since the look that might or might not have been a look, look. *Naked Grace.* By the time she got to the elevator bank, only Brassard was left standing, rather leaning, against the chrome door trim. He had an open beer can in his hand and another tucked in his pants pocket.

"Thaaat waaasss fuunny," he slurred.

Yaz looked around for someone to answer, but they were alone as the elevator doors shut behind them. "What was?" She knew she'd regret asking.

"Donahue talking about love. That girl's a dyke. No offense."

Yaz could not imagine how on earth she could not be offended by the oddly backhanded slur. She knew she presented as a butch, or at least on the androgenous end of the butch spectrum. She didn't try to hide who she was. Ever. And mostly, she didn't care what people thought. Silence was probably the best response now, and it worked perfectly because she had no words. He stepped closer to her, the stench of beer and ignorance filling her personal space. It reminded her of the incident she'd had as an apprentice. That jerk, her boss at the time, had also been drunk and had the nerve to tell her he could "make her a real woman." Yaz took a step away from Brassard.

"She totally is," he continued, ignoring Yaz's retreat. "A buddy of mine took her out once. Said she was as frigid as the arctic. Shame, really." He pursed his lips and squinted his eyes, giving her an almost comical tip to toe. "I think she's into you. She's so fuckin' hot, right? I mean, those legs…" He blinked and then looked down again at Yaz's legs. "You've got some nice legs too, lady. How tall are you? Doesn't happen often with your people. Well, I guess Yao Ming maybe…"

Once Yaz got past being called "lady," she realized she wasn't sure what kind of insult he'd intended. Gender? Race? Sexuality? Basketball? All unclear. The only word that would've pushed her more quickly over the edge would've been if he'd called her "exotic." But he'd nonetheless come too close. Drunk or not drunk. As the door to his floor opened, her tiger pounced. She pushed him out with enough force that he stumbled backwards and fell flat on his back. The beer in his hand emptied on the way down and soaked his shirt thoroughly. The one in his pocket burst on impact with the floor, soaking his pants with a spray of lager.

"Shut up you racist, sexist, homophobic piece of shit." She was too angry to defend basketball.

"Me likey when a woman gets rough…"

It was all Yaz could do not to launch at him, but she knew that people who used slurs so readily were beyond ignorant, and nothing she wanted to do to Brassard in that moment would shake it out of him. Instead, she drew a shaky breath to calm herself, and through clenched teeth let her words do the punching. "You know something, Brassard, it may surprise you to know that not only do I have less than zero interest in satisfying your Asian fetishisms, I am also bad at math. And I'm a great driver, so make sure you look both ways when crossing the street from now on. Fair warning."

The doors slowly slid together. After a breath or two, she managed to calm herself. After all, she'd certainly had ignorance volleyed her way before, and she wasn't going to let Brassard's objectifying comments land within the lines. What she was having more trouble dismissing was his suggestion that Grace was gay. Not that it mattered one way or the other. *Or did it?* It would be nice if she was on the team. *Was that really a wink, then?* She was gorgeous. *Now you're objectifying.* Why would any of this matter? Grace Donahue was the competition even if she was on the same team. *Is that even possible?* Yaz stepped out on her floor, grateful that the metal doors had barricaded her perplexing thoughts behind them.

CHAPTER TEN

Round Two, Day Four

Grace had just finished lacing up her sneakers, intent on going to run stairs, when she heard a knock on the suite door.

"I got it!" Yaz bounded from her room into the foyer and almost straight into Grace. "Sorry!" She peeked through the peephole and stepped back, opening the door.

"Hey, Tiff," Grace said. "We weren't expecting you today. Not that it isn't lovely to see you." She wondered what brought her by on Day Four. "We both had our interviews already this morning."

"Is it some kind of surprise?" Yaz asked with an almost childlike glee. "Where are we going?"

Tiff held a hand up to hold back the enthusiasm, and Grace could tell she wasn't there with good news.

"Come in, have a seat," Grace said, ushering her into the living room.

"Yeah, Tiff, what's up? Is something wrong?"

"Yaz, we got a call from Jenni."

Grace saw Yaz grab the back of the couch.

"Oh my God, Tiff, is it my mom? Is she okay?"

Grace stepped beside Yaz and put an arm around her back.

"Your mom is fine, but the producers have sanctioned a family phone call."

Tiff handed Yaz a cell phone and she held it like it was a grenade. Grace put her hand on Yaz's wrist to steady her. "Why don't you go give Jenni a call?" she said, gesturing toward the bedrooms. "Tiff and I will wait here, right, Tiff?"

Tiff nodded. "Take your time."

When Yaz's door was closed, Grace offered Tiff a drink.

"What do you have that's hard?" she asked, setting her clipboard down.

"Whoa. You're asking for liquor, and you just put your clipboard down for the first time since we met. Is this thing with Yaz that bad?"

"No. I mean, maybe not. I only know that someone close to her is, I dunno…missing?"

Grace set a beer on the kitchen island in front of Tiff. "Like, missing missing? That can't be good."

"Honestly, all I know is that when the call came in from, er, Jenni…?" She looked down at the clipboard. "Yes, Jenni. Jenni called, and Perry and Bette both decided the situation, whatever it is, warranted Yaz's attention. Hopefully, it's nothing too serious."

Grace could hear Yaz's voice coming from the bedroom. It sounded strained, higher somehow. Panicked maybe? There were several moments of brief silence, presumably when Jenni was talking, and then a much longer silence after which Yaz came out of the bedroom. She wasn't making eye contact, looking down at the phone in her hand instead. She walked slowly at first, then her pace picked up and only when she reached the kitchen island did she raise her eyes, and only to Tiff. She set the phone down.

"Are you—" Tiff began.

"Yes, yes, it's okay. Uh. Things are fine."

"Seriously?" Tiff sounded as surprised as Grace felt.

"Yeah, just a moment of panic by my cousin, but nothing she can't work out on her own."

Yaz said the words with just enough conviction to convince Tiff, but Grace wasn't buying it. Something about how her eyes were darting around the room, looking almost everywhere except in Grace's direction. She wasn't physically pacing back and forth, but that's the sense that Grace got from her demeanor. Like a caged animal.

Yaz started walking toward the foyer. "So, thanks for the phone call, Tiff."

Tiff took the hint and slugged back the remainder of her beer, picked up her clipboard and the phone, and followed. "No problem, Yaz, but listen, if you need anything, you just let me know, okay?"

"Thanks. No worries."

Grace was astonished by the oddness of the exchange. Yaz sounded almost robotic, like she was trying to exorcise emotion from her voice. Once Tiff had gone, Yaz walked into her bedroom and closed the door behind her.

Well, that was very weird.

Maybe there was no cause for worry. Probably this was none of her business, and if Yaz wanted to share, she would. But why had Yaz refused to acknowledge her presence? She thought they'd bonded over the past couple of days. Certainly nothing contentious had happened between them. Her thoughts flashed to the dressing of Yaz's wound. And to that moment in the pantry. *Those weren't nothing.* Not only did she feel something pass between them, but she knew Yaz felt it too. Or maybe she just hoped? And what was with the tattoo?

She was so curious where the tiger-striped tail led. Given its dimensions, if the whole cat was under Yaz's sleeve, it must take up most of her arm. She wondered if it hurt Yaz when it was inked. Of course, it did. Did she have others? What were they? Where were they? And why was she thinking about this when clearly something about Yaz was off?

Grace was standing in the foyer when Yaz's bedroom door opened. She blushed, feeling as though her thoughts had penetrated the door and magically lured the tiger out. But Yaz's mood hadn't changed much from when Tiff was there. She did manage to meet Grace's eyes this time, though briefly, before announcing in that same robotic voice that she was going for a walk around the hotel and would be back soon. She gave Grace no time to ask questions before the door closed behind her.

❖

Yaz was conscious of three things as she made her way down the hotel stairwell. The thumping of blood in her ears as panic surged from her heart. Her mom's voice, reminding her as it regularly did not to act impulsively. And the words "Sabrina is missing."

"What do you mean missing?" she'd recalled saying to Jenni minutes ago, before leaving the penthouse.

"She didn't show for her shift last night, or this morning," Jenni had explained. "The shelter called me asking if I'd seen her. She's not answering her phone. Yaz, don't panic. I'm on prep shift this morning, but I'll go check her apartment as soon as I'm done here at the restaurant."

Jenni's voice was calm, but Yaz had detected a slight warble that signaled that her cousin shared a similar fear.

"When did you see her last? And what was her mood?"

"I dunno, Yaz. A bit quiet, maybe? Hard to know."

"Why hard to know?" Yaz wasn't imagining it. Jenni was keeping something from her.

"Jeez. Okay. She's been a bit busy. It's the third week of the month, so the numbers at the shelter have ramped up a bit. And…"

"And I'm not there." End of month was when the aid checks came in, and the week before was always tough for people living rough because they were often running on empty. *Fuck.*

"Yaz, you're not the only volunteer in that kitchen. The person who was supposed to work your shifts came down with summer COVID. I've been filling in as best I can and…" Jenni trailed off, but Yaz knew she could tell exactly what she was thinking. "Cousin, seriously, save your worry until there's something to worry about. I should make it to her place in less than an hour. I'll call you back then."

Jenni left no room for Yaz to protest. What Jenni probably didn't know was that Yaz had already immersed herself in worry and self-recrimination. Why had she chosen to come on the show? She knew from her dad's failures that sobriety was challenging, even for those who'd made it as long as Sabrina had without a drink. Constant vigilance and a strict adherence to the program were absolutes. Dry drunks had their own set of challenges, and even though Yaz's dad hadn't made it to any level of recovery, she knew from Al-Anon that behavioral and mood changes were markers to keep an eye on. Sabrina hadn't missed a shift since Yaz had started working with her four years ago. And she wasn't usually quiet. Even when busy. And she was busy because of her.

Sabrina's apartment wasn't going to be first on her list of places to look. If she was starting to slide, she'd likely go looking for old friends from her drinking days. She remembered that McCalley's in the east end had been her favorite hole, so that's where she'd check first. Again, though, her mom's voice was in her head. Be patient, Tiger. She was already in the stairwell and halfway to the ground floor when it occurred to her what the personal cost might be if she was caught leaving.

Patience was not a trait she had mastered. Far from it. The tiger on her arm, a tattoo she'd bought with some insurance money left by her dad, was meant as a reminder to stay ready and assess situations before deciding to pounce. Because that's what Yaz did. That's what she'd always done. Reactiveness was her go-to. And yes, she had to admit that sometimes it was a character flaw. She knew it made relationships difficult. She'd jump in too soon. Or lose patience when things got uncomfortable. When people got too close. But the tiger mnemonic was drowned out by the panic she was feeling, and as she reached the ground floor, she could only think about Sabrina. Was she okay? Maybe. It wasn't like her to miss a shift. Maybe things were completely fine, and she'd lost her phone. Or maybe she was under the weather. It could be a million things. Or one.

She cautiously stepped out of the stairwell, checking to make sure no one associated with the show was in sight. No point in advertising her presence. With any luck, she'd be back before anyone noticed her absence. All clear.

A sign for Shipping and Receiving, with an arrow pointing down a hallway, came into sight. She approached the door at the end and her hand trembled as she put it on the metal push bar, looking around to make sure she'd not been seen. Her mouth went pasty dry. *Sabrina is missing.* She swallowed against the panic, knowing that her fear of getting caught leaving the hotel was nothing compared to her fear for her mentor.

❖

It was hard not to notice a cloudless spring day in Vancouver. The mountains erupted across the harbor as Yaz turned onto Denman Street, but the exceptional weather barely registered except for a moment of gratitude that it wasn't raining, because she hadn't thought in her haste to bring a jacket. And without her phone, using a ride-sharing app was out of the question. Even the usually hypnotic aroma of roasting beans from her favorite coffee shop didn't slow her pace. It might normally have taken her an hour to walk to the neighborhood near Cambie Street, but she cut down toward the Bayshore and zigzagged over toward West Hastings in order to dodge some of the tourist traffic. She arrived at McCalley's in just under forty minutes. Nothing like panic to put pep in one's step. And that's how she felt. Like she was reliving the day she went looking for her dad. But this was Sabrina. Her mentor. Her friend. The bar door looked like something out of Medieval times—distressed thick planks suspended by tarnished hand-hammered tee hinges. She swallowed hard and pulled back on the forged iron door handle, then stepped into the dark.

It took a moment for her eyes to adjust. She scanned the bar, which looked exactly as she'd expected from its name. Emerald green leather seats covering well-worn wooden stools lined a bar that ran pretty much the length of the whole space. Irish flags and soccer banners were plastered on the low ceilings, and the walls were covered with posters that included the Derry Girls, graffiti proclaiming *Sinéad Go Deo*, *Guinness*

Is Good For You, and, in disproportionately large font *Irish Is The Only Whiskey!*

"Damn it, Yaz. What are you doing here?"

The voice echoed in the murky stillness, filling her with relief. "I could ask you the same thing."

Yaz moved toward the far end of the bar and plunked down on the stool beside Sabrina. Without hesitation, she picked up the old-fashioned glass that sat in front of her and smelled its contents. "Vanilla. Orange. Jameson?"

"Gold Reserve. Very good nose, Yaz."

"How does it taste?"

"I don't remember."

Yaz turned in her seat and put a hand on Sabrina's, tugging at it slightly until their eyes met. She weighed the emotions she saw there. "You don't, do you." It was more a statement than question.

"Haven't touched it." Sabrina waved toward a tall wavy-haired man standing near the cash register at the far end of the bar. "Jimmy?" she said.

As if expecting the question, almost as if he'd been in this situation a hundred times before, he looked Yaz straight in the eye and said, "She hasn't touched it. Didn't last night either. Not a drop."

Even without Jimmy weighing in, Yaz knew it was true. "Why?"

"Why here? Why sitting in a bar staring at a glass of whiskey?"

"Yes, Sabrina, what is going on?" Yaz asked the question with as much tenderness as she could. Shaming and judgment had no place in the moment, and she knew it. *Give her time.*

"For some reason I needed to test myself."

"Some reason?"

Sabrina took a deep breath and stared straight ahead, letting her lungs slowly release as she shook her head. "I ran into an old drinking buddy at the shelter yesterday. He's living rough. Looking rough. High. I saw myself. Scared myself, I guess."

"He's not you. Not now."

"No, he's not. I'm not white-knuckling, Yaz. I just felt, I dunno, guilty maybe. That I'm clean."

Yaz was relieved to hear that Sabrina wasn't craving alcohol, but her choice to come to a bar and put herself in harm's way wasn't ideal. "You're aware that what you're doing here may not be the best idea, right? Have you been to a meeting this week?"

"No. But I'm aware that I should go. And I will. Just because I'm sober doesn't mean I have it all figured out. I need to deal with this every day."

Yaz reflected on her experience with her dad, who as far as she knew, had never admitted to anyone, including himself, that he had an addiction problem. It was no real surprise that together with his mental health issues and fed by the shame he felt because of his business failings, his substance abuse had intensified and expanded. After he'd passed, she'd educated herself through various family support programs and was now much better versed on what to listen for. Sabrina was having no trouble communicating. Nor was she showing any anger or resentment, or feelings of victimization. All good signs. But she'd endangered herself, her sobriety, by being in this bar. Yaz needed to get her out, of her own accord.

Yaz probed further. "Anything else?"

"I oversalted the chili this week. Seriously. When have I ever done that?"

"Not the worst crime."

"You know we can't afford those kinds of mistakes. We run things pretty lean, as you know."

Yaz did know. Funding for the kitchen was partially subsidized by the local government, the rest from public donation. Those sources kept them running but didn't consider additional overhead costs for things like equipment. They'd just recently lost one of the chest freezers to old age, and another was filled with more frost than food. Even with her lack of budgeting acumen, she could tell that eventually things would grind to a halt. Fuck. It dawned on her that she might have ended the one hope she had for preventing that from happening. She shifted uncomfortably in her seat, and Sabrina was quick to notice.

"Yaz, why are you here? I mean, aren't you supposed to be sequestered at the hotel? Tell me you didn't..."

"It's okay, they know." Yaz hated to lie, but at least it was partly true and that was enough to quell suspicion. The producers knew there was a problem. They just didn't know she'd gone to fix it. And she was almost there. Just one more thing. She pushed back from the bar and slipped off the stool. "How about you and I go find a meeting?"

"How about we do that?" Sabrina smiled.

❖

Some walk.

Grace had put in an hour on the stairs, showered and dressed, then spent another hour walking around the hotel with the hope of running into Yaz. She'd finally given up and landed back in the suite with an hour to kill before dinner. Yaz was right. The couch was everything a couch should be.

A sound at the door woke her up. She leapt up and was relieved to see Yaz standing in the foyer, flipping the key card in her fingers as if doing a card trick.

"Are you okay?" Grace asked.

She stepped out of her boots, set the card on the entranceway table, and expelled a lungful of air with such volume that it pulled her shoulders down with it.

"I'm fucked."

She came and sat in one of the chairs facing the couch, pulled her feet up, and hugged her knees.

"Yaz, what is going on? Please tell me?"

"You'll be one competitor down by the end of the day. Earlier if you let them know now."

"I don't understand. Tell who what now?"

"I left. I mean, I left the hotel property. All afternoon. I was somewhere else."

Grace hesitated. This was not good. Very not good. The contestant contracts made it clear that violating any rule of the contest could result in expulsion from the show. And the sequestering rule had a whole page of its own in the contract. It was a big bold capitalized letters rule. Yaz must've had a good reason to violate it, and there was no point dwelling on a fait accompli. Grace accepted it as a sign of progress that Yaz considered her trustworthy enough to confide. It sure beat silence.

"Did anyone see you leave?"

Yaz looked a bit stunned by the question. "I left by the loading doors. I don't think anyone saw me. If they did, well..." She turned her head and raised her sleeve to wipe her eyes. "I had no choice."

Grace walked into the kitchen, hoping to give Yaz some space and time to decompress. She went into the fridge and pulled out a couple of Steamworks Flagship IPAs and poured them into a couple of tulip glasses before returning to the couch. Yaz was at the window, chewing on a fingernail. Grace set the beer on the coffee table and patted the seat beside her. "Come sit. Tell me what happened. I'm guessing it had something to do with the phone call?"

Yaz eyed the beer and plunked herself in front of it.

"It was Jenni, my contact person." Yaz saw a brief flash of surprise on Grace's face. "She's my cousin. She got a call this morning from the shelter we volunteer at, Safe Harbor, asking if she or I might know where Sabrina was. Apparently, she hadn't shown up for the dinner shift, or breakfast this morning. She's not like that. Normally."

Grace thought it was an odd ending to the explanation, and it must've shown on her face because Yaz immediately clarified.

"She's dependable." Yaz took a drink and then stared at the glass in her hand.

"So the no-show raised concerns?"

"Sabrina has been sober for over four years. It wasn't an easy four years. Some people never get there. My dad didn't. Not once, though he must've made a million promises. He never asked for help. It's like he wanted to hurt. When he wanted to hurt more, he made us hurt more. I wanted to fix things. But I couldn't. I couldn't sit here and hope that Sabrina wasn't making the same choices my dad did. I just couldn't."

Yaz shook her head emphatically as she put her beer on the table and pushed it back from her.

Grace did likewise. "What happened to Sabrina?" Given what had happened with Yaz's dad, she was afraid of what the answer might be.

"Jenni was working so I had to go find her. I did. At a bar down on Hastings."

"Was she…had she…" Grace didn't know how to ask.

"She was staring at a glass on the bar in front of her. Whiskey. She'd done the same thing the night before."

"Staring? Not drinking?"

"Not drinking. Just wanted to test herself. Was going through some stuff."

"Yaz, that's great, right?"

"Wasn't an ideal strategy, but she agreed to go to a meeting. And that was great. I walked her there and waited 'til it was over. Her sponsor was there too, so I left her in good hands. But not before she bawled me out for probably ruining my chances at winning this thing."

"And if you haven't ruined your chances? Like, if nobody saw you leave…" Grace put a hand on Yaz's leg and squeezed to gain her full attention, "you'll still have to beat me with our next dishes, my friend."

Yaz laughed and she threw herself back into the couch pillows. When she righted herself, a lock of hair fell from the tousled mess on top of her head and dangled in front of her left eye. Grace, having seen Yaz do it dozens of times, instinctively reached for it and tucked it back into the chaos. *Perfect.* She paused, leaving her fingers to hang in the space between them. Why had she never noticed her mouth? Her flawless skin? Of course, she'd noticed the hair. Shaved sides but dark thick length on top. A bit like Miley Cyrus during one of her gender-fluid hair phases. Messy but controlled, the style accentuated Yaz's narrow facial structure and high cheekbones. Curiosity had taken control of her fingers and they were now brushing along the shaved side just above Yaz's ear.

"I love your hair. I couldn't pull it off myself, but it suits you perfectly."

Yaz shifted slightly but didn't pull away. "It's all about the product. Gels. Pastes. Sprays. I could well be flammable." She smiled and Grace felt a flame rush up her arm. "You may have noticed I keep myself a good distance back from open flame cooktops."

"I'll try to remember that."

Grace froze. This was that moment, she realized. That moment when everything looked like it was being filmed through a soft filter. When sound dulled because your blood was pounding in your ears, and other places south of the border. And you forgot where exactly you were because nothing else existed. Except the lips in front of you. Lips you so badly wanted to kiss.

"I hope I didn't burn myself by breaking the rules today. If I did, it was worth it."

Clearly, Yaz was not in the same moment with Grace. *Understandably.*

"No one will hear it from me," Grace said, trying not to be disappointed while wondering if that moment would ever return. *Should* ever return. After all, they were adversaries. "Speaking of rules, I tried again to get us into a suite on one of the lower floors. Mr. Barney said something will come available in a day or two. I hope that's okay."

"It is." Yaz took a final swig of beer. "But I hate giving up this joint given how long we're planning on being here."

Grace felt relief when Yaz winked and laughed. It was better that they'd reestablished a comfortable boundary. For them both. *Wasn't it?*

CHAPTER ELEVEN

Round Three, Day One

Yaz woke up the next day feeling hopeful. Today they'd learn what the next central ingredient would be, and as she dressed for the day, she tried to imagine which of the innumerable foods they'd be assigned. Living in British Columbia her whole life, she felt incredibly fortunate for the abundance and variety available. Pacific seafood, fruits and vegetables, vineyards and breweries. From shoreline to mountains and valleys, the province had it all. And while it still boggled her mind that food insecurity existed, she maintained the belief that it was within the community's power to change the dynamic. This television show was giving her the opportunity to move the needle in the right direction. Her hopefulness lasted for five minutes.

Tiff wasn't alone when she arrived at the suite. With her were Bette and Perry.

This can't be good.

It was obvious by the producers' expressions—well, Bette's really because Perry wore a perma-scowl—that something was up and Yaz sensed it had something to do with her. And yesterday's situation. They almost ignored Grace, who was sitting in one of the living room chairs cherishing her morning coffee.

"We need to talk," Perry growled.

Bette nodded toward Grace, then tilted her head at Perry. "How about we go out to the balcony?" She'd stressed "we" and gestured in a way that made it clear Grace was not invited.

They stepped through the sliding doors and Tiff pulled them closed behind them.

"It has come to our attention, Yaz, that yesterday afternoon you left the hotel property. Is that true?" Perry was humorless. *Consistent.*

"It is. I did." There was no point denying it, and while owning her actions gave Yaz a sense of relief, it was heavily mixed with fear, frustration, and anger. Fear about what the consequences would be, and the latter two emotions elbowing each other out of the way to shoot imaginary arrows straight through the balcony windows and into Grace. She couldn't really expect her to keep her secret, though, could she? Was that fair? Hells yes, it was full on fair. She should be mad. After all, Grace had promised exactly that. "No one will hear it from me," she'd said. And then there was the disappointment. What was the point of any of it? The promise? The kindness? The touching? Yaz suddenly felt like a little yellow tennis ball. Why did she tell her in the first place? What was she thinking letting Grace touch her? It wasn't even a kiss, though Yaz had hardly slept last night imagining how soft her damn lips would've been. How the spot just below her perfect damn ear along her perfect damn neck would've tasted. She'd never find out. Grace had played her. Game. Set. Match.

"Yaz?" Bette's voice slowed the deluge of thoughts that flowed through her head. "Did this have something to do with the phone call we received yesterday?"

She didn't want to be intentionally evasive, but protecting Sabrina would always be her priority. Her mentor's reputation had already been dragged through the mud and she wasn't going to unfairly add to them. "I expect you'll be sending me home?"

"Are you aware," Perry said, obviously dissatisfied with Yaz's response, "that your actions could've jeopardized the whole series? There's a reason we have that codicil in the contracts, and you've given us license to do exactly that. Send you home—"

"—but," Bette didn't let Perry continue, "in light of the fact that neither you nor any of the contestants have yet been told this round's ingredient, your actions did not give you any substantive advantage. So you will not be sent home."

What?

"However, for Round Three, you will compete with the minimum featured ingredient. We will edit footage taken at the location shoot so that it appears you simply fell short gathering your ingredient."

"We'll add an addendum to your NDA, which you will have to re-sign. And you will not be given a tablet this round." Perry emphasized this by taking one of the digital notepads Tiff held and tucking it under her arm.

"Next time, please think twice," said Bette.

"*Next* time will be your *last*," added Perry as she turned to leave.

Once the producers were gone, Tiff shared that the round's ingredients would be goat's milk and cheese.

"One hour," she said, handing the single tablet to Grace before leaving the suite.

Grace stared at her tablet, then at Yaz. "What just happened?"

Yaz's relief at not being thrown out turned sour as she contemplated how to respond. "They know."

"How?"

Yaz felt her cheeks burn. *Is this what betrayal feels like?*

"They didn't say, Grace." Very heavy on the *Grace*. "They didn't have to, did they? Only you and I knew I'd gone out."

"Yaz, you don't think that I…" she paused, blinking with the realization. "Well, obviously you do.'

Obviously. And don't blink your mesmerizing damn eyes at me.

Any question Yaz might have had about whose team Grace played on was answered yesterday when her baby blues had darkened with desire. Not that she, or anyone had to pick a team. *But awesome. Sexy.* Fuck. Why was she thinking about this? How could she have let down her guard and forgotten it was a competition? Because Grace hadn't. She was playing hard. Proof positive that the apple doesn't fall far from the tree, no matter how it bounces. Once a Donahue, always a Donahue.

"Yaz, I wouldn't betray your confidence. You don't know me well enough, but I—"

"You're right. I don't know you." She thought about what Lyn Sanyal had told her about Grace's single-mindedness. Of course she'd do anything to win. "But for some reason I can't comprehend—given who you are—you want to win this competition no matter what you have to do."

Grace stepped back. "I'm going to ignore that, Yaz. Now tell me what happened."

Yaz hadn't heard Grace speak so forcefully before, but her own anger had taken the wheel now and there was no turning around. "What did you think was going to happen?!"

"Well, honestly, I thought you'd be shown the door, but you're still here so—"

"Yes. I am still here," Yaz shifted to a higher gear. "Sorry to disappoint you."

Grace sighed as if defeated. "Okay. You're mad. I get it. Here's the plan. I'm going to use the tablet for half the hour given, and then you're going to take it. No one said we couldn't share."

Yaz put her foot to the floor. "I didn't come from your world, *as you know*, but I don't need your pity. Or charity." She hopped over the back of the couch, consumed by her anger, irritated by the inescapable scent of snickerdoodles and oddly aware of the heated tiles beneath her feet as she strode to her room.

"Don't make things worse for yourself, Yaz. Please."

Slam.

"Fine, I'll slip it under your door when I'm done."

CHAPTER TWELVE

Round Three, Day Two

Misery. That's what the day had been. Yaz wondered how that was possible, given that most of the time she'd been surrounded by the sweetest most goofy-eyed little animals she'd ever seen.

It had started off rocky, with a turbulent but thankfully short plane ride to Salt Spring, the largest of Vancouver's neighboring Gulf Islands. En route, she'd stared below at the Salish Sea, the enormous body of water that surrounded the San Juan and Gulf Islands and flowed from Campbell River in the north all the way down to Olympia, Washington. Most people chose to travel to the cluster of islands on the ferry from Tsawwassen on the mainland into Salt Spring's Fulford Harbour, but the plane saved the contestants and crew almost four hours each way. She'd thought back to Perry's opening speech to the contestants, about time being money. When Grace had been late. *Not late*. She had been drawn to her that day. Irresistibly cute. Impossibly sweet. Deceptively deceptive.

"Did you know that most people think Vancouver, the city, is on Vancouver, the island?" Kaley had chirped at one point.

The question had proved rhetorical, Yaz surmised, because most of the remaining competitors had been too busy grabbing the edges of their seats to talk much. Yaz's silence was different, as she was consumed with the kind of self-loathing she knew wasn't going to benefit her in the long run. But as the plane bumped along, she couldn't help but wallow. Trusting Grace with her secret was mistake number one. Sharing details with her about Sabrina, and her dad, was an unforgiveable mistake number two. She knew she needed to focus on the second chance she'd been given, but she had built herself a mountain and was struggling to find a way to climb it.

Once at the goat farm, they'd been given a short demonstration of milking the does and then provided with a stable of the surprisingly clean and curious beasts. The camera, lighting, and sound operators moved through the barn slowly, trying not to disturb the animals as they gathered audio and video for the episode. For the most part, she'd become immune to them, learning to dodge them during the studio kitchen scenes with surprising ease. She'd set to the task, knowing that while her punishment was going to make it hard, winning was still possible. As she'd pulled on the milk-swollen glands, extracting the pungent liquid—most of which ended up on her clothes—Yaz had taken a moment to look around the barn.

Brassard was cursing his way through the task with a look of disgust as he squirted himself repeatedly. When he looked up and saw Yaz, he stopped and stared wordlessly back at her, a sneer tugging at the corner of his thin lips. *Jerk.* But at least he was keeping his dumb mouth shut. Kew and Kaley were laughing over their own efforts, cheering when the occasional stream of milk pinged off the inside of the metal bucket. Francine was intently hunched over her bucket, hands and fingers working diligently on her beast, while doing her best to ignore Vij's efforts to squirt her with his animal's output. Grace was…well, she was nowhere to be seen. The film crew had also disappeared. Yaz had cursed herself for her curiosity, but since she was going to be docked part of her bounty anyways, figured it wouldn't hurt to go see where they'd gone.

As she'd walked toward the stable doors, she saw a cluster of cameras pointing out toward the yard. A cacophony of bleating and familiar laughter grew louder. She stopped beside one of the boom operators and turned to the sound. Grace was running in circles with outstretched arms, chasing a small group of pygmy goats around the enclosure. A rope trailed behind one of the tiny animals, but it was hard to tell which. Mud and hay were flying around the hoard, Grace in mad pursuit and covered with the debris, but all the while, laughing. Then she'd slipped and fallen butt-first into a puddle. She'd continued to giggle, wrapping her arms around muddied jeans as if trying to contain her delight as the animals—probably realizing she was no longer a threat—surrounded her, butting their heads against her seated form. Then she'd turned to the camera and flashed that smile. That million-dollar trust fund smile. Yaz had felt the crew vibrating with triumph. It had been quite a display. Made for TV. When Grace had turned her sights toward Yaz, she'd immediately ducked back into the barn.

Her self-recrimination turned outward when Grace rejoined her and the other milkers and set about refilling her pail. *Who does she think she is? Tee-hee! Look how cute they are!* Bah. Ripped-knee jeans? *Poser.* When did it become cool to mimic those who had no choice but to wear ripped clothes?

Jesus, Yaz, you need to calm the fuck down. Tay Tay's more PG lyrics flipped through her head, and the melody followed. Inexplicably, it was strangely soothing.

The remainder of their time at the goat farm had been spent watching the milk being processed into the tangy cylinders that would eventually age into the creamy cheese that Salt Spring was known for, including the final step of decorating the top with aromatics and tiny edible flowers. From an aesthetic and flavor perspective, the end product was an indisputably perfect highlight for any charcuterie board, and a flexible ingredient for either sweet or savory dishes. Yaz's creative juices had churned as she considered tomorrow's impossibly challenging dish, giving her some much-needed respite from the day's otherwise petty and bitter thoughts.

On the flight back, she'd again gazed out across the gulf waters that stretched below, hoping to catch sight of the Haida Gwaii islands well to the north of their flight path. As a child, she'd gone there with her parents on summer holiday to take in the wildlife. She still remembered the incredible variety and number of birds, enormous and playful sea lions, and one enormous black bear that had plodded along the side of the road they'd been traveling on one evening. Her dad had explained that the islands, known to some as the Canadian Galapagos, were host to a unique species of bear that had evolved specifically so that it could eat through tough mollusks and crabs. Yaz hadn't eaten either since without thinking about the island's top predator, whose head was bigger than a basketball.

She thought about that bear now, reminding herself that she also wanted to be top of a different sort of food chain. Winning could do a lot for her family and community. It would clear debts so that she could afford to bring her mom back to Canada, for a visit or maybe even to stay depending how well her auntie was doing. And to keep the soup kitchen operating by buying some much-needed new appliances. To do that, she needed to win. And to win, she needed to stay focused and create exceptional dishes.

Yaz felt pretty sure she could achieve the first by keeping a distance from Grace and putting a lid on the flutters that tickled her stomach when she was around. Easy compared to the second requirement. Creating an outstanding dish this week with the minimal amount of product she had been given to highlight—a quart of goat's milk and a half pound of cheese, less than a third of what the others procured—was going to be nothing but misery.

❖

Round Three, Day Three

Brutal. That's the only way Grace could describe Round Three. Every aspect of her dish had gone horribly wrong. She'd been called first to the kitchen, and for ten minutes felt uncomfortable in the relative solitude. Her confidence in the dish she'd chosen, a seasoned tangy goat cheese souffle, should have carried her through.

She'd made the delicate fluffy egg classic so many times with success that she'd believed the discord between her and Yaz couldn't deflate her hopes. But as soon as Yaz appeared, in the time slot immediately after hers, she realized she was wrong. Just like in the lobby and on the bus earlier this morning, Yaz had refused to acknowledge Grace when they'd crossed paths on set. Sure, she'd expected the rebuff today, but it still hurt.

In response, she'd overcompensated and found herself overly focused, if that was possible, on her technique and the orderliness of her station. Her incessant self-criticism and efforts to avoid distraction had backfired. Don't think about a black horse, she'd thought. And then the inevitable stampede of black horses had caused her to lose track of the roux's timing and she'd undercooked it. Fortunately, the bechamel was smooth, but the judges didn't miss the slip, commenting that she'd been lucky the cheesy sauce had held up the egg whites for an "acceptable aeration." Her plating, though, had been boring. Her seasonings unbalanced. When had nutmeg ever betrayed her? It was impossible that she'd move on after the judges' scathing reviews. She sat in the Stew 'n' Brew with the others, waiting to be called for the summary and elimination.

In the greenroom, her own distress was topped up by Yaz's silent treatment, and it wasn't possible she could be sitting further away. Grace couldn't entirely blame her since she was the only one Yaz had confided in about leaving the hotel. But she'd hoped that their developing relationship would continue. Was it even a relationship? Technically no. Friendship? Maybe yes? Now, though, whatever it was had come to a screeching halt. Nonetheless, she'd wished for the benefit of the doubt. She would never have violated her confidence that way. More hurtful than the silent treatment, though, had been Yaz's indictment that she'd pitied her. And a charity case? Neither were true, but they'd gotten under her skin. Deeply. They reminded her of all that can go wrong with power and privilege. Maybe it was impossible to discuss and there was no way to fix it. Something needed to shift, and until then, there would just be hurt feelings.

Everyone seemed in a mood. Christian was sulking. Kaley was atypically quiet. Francine hadn't come back from the smoking area since her review. Vij and Kew seemed low, but the Canucks lost their game last night, and that seemed of more concern than their individual feedback. By the time the judges called the group out for their final decision, there were more than the usual number of empty beer bottles on the table. By the time they returned to the hotel afterward, Grace was thankful that no one was required to drive, and that it was a single elimination week. Francine had somehow managed to serve up something even less palatable than her own dish— lemon goat yogurt entremet that puckered the mouths of half the judges—and was sent home.

Yaz's dish was spectacular, from the sounds of it. The guest judge, Tam Williamson, claimed it was the best gelato she'd ever eaten. Grace missed hearing the details from Yaz directly and hoped that eventually the truth would come to light and they'd be talking again.

Back at the hotel, Yaz was first off the bus and already in the elevator by the time Grace walked into the lobby. As she passed the security desk, she noticed a small row of monitors. Of course! The hotel had security cameras. She found her way to Shipping and Receiving and stepped outside the doorway. She scanned the corners and roof eaves until she found what she was looking for. But the camera was pointing toward the gate at the end of the loading area, and the pedestrian exit seemed too far from the camera's range. Grace guessed the producers didn't see Yaz leave on camera. She looked up at the building again, hoping to find another camera that could explain things. Instead, she caught movement in a guestroom window on the side of the building with no balconies. Christian Brassard was looking down at her from the window. He lifted the beer he held in his hand to her as if to toast, then smiled and walked away.

Bingo. It had to be him. Who else would be so petty and mean?

Grace was elated. She was sure that once she told Yaz about Christian's view of the docks, she'd be off the hook that Yaz had set her on. And Christian would be on it. She couldn't prove it though. Not really. Even with the self-satisfied smirk he'd flashed, it could be coincidence. He had the view and the mean spirit. Means and motive. Still. Circumstantial at best. Her excitement came to a quick and excruciating halt. She needed proof. But she could still tell Yaz about his view, couldn't she? Her mind volleyed the fairness question back and forth, and she wondered what she could say to vindicate herself without accusing Christian. She stopped at the lobby shop to pick up some of the foil-wrapped chocolates Yaz loved, still undecided about what she would say.

When she got to the room, Yaz's door was closed, and she could hear the shower coming from inside. She allowed herself a moment to think about what Yaz would look like naked, warm water running across her soft tattooed skin. Through the dark wavy hair and down the long, smooth neck. She held her breath and imagined standing with her, their bodies soapy, pressed together. What the hell was going on with her libido lately? Maybe it was just the relief she felt in knowing that she and Yaz would be back on solid ground again. Hopefully soon. Wow, though. It had just been so long since her body tingled the way it was tingling right now. Clearly, she needed to work off some nervous energy. Yes. That's what it was. Nervous energy. She left the chocolates on the foyer table with a note that read, "Sweets for the sweet," then quickly changed into her tennis gear and headed to the courts.

Grace had grown up playing tennis, and at first, was ambivalent about the sport. Part of that was because at eleven years old, she'd wanted nothing more than to play softball. That opportunity had ended the minute her mother caught her looking at the shortstop for the local team with a bit more than sporting interest. Or as her mom put it, the "wrong kind of interest." Grace didn't understand the comment then, given that at that age, she hadn't developed any conscious understanding of her sexual self. It wasn't until the grade-twelve prom, when the group dance she and Joss had been shuffling to transitioned to a slow groove. "Stay," Joss had said. Grace had, and under the twinkling lights of the school gym-turned-dance floor, everything about her world—their world—had changed. Then eight years later, tragically, it had changed again.

Grace set her stance and pounded the ball to the opposite court. Tennis had become therapy. She imagined that each ball came with a memory and with each hit, though it might look to others like she was beating it down, in her heart, she was dispatching it into the universe. Setting it free into forever. She'd learned from grief counseling that getting over Joss's death wasn't healthy but getting through it was. There were times when she was, admittedly, better at it than others. So she continued to practice, each time knowing she was nearing the other side. Getting through it.

As she continued her routine, she realized that Yaz reminded her of Joss. Maybe that accounted for the strange familiarity she'd been feeling. The two of them were different physically, Yaz being taller and leaner. But they both had a fearless quality. Yaz appeared as impulsive as Joss, too, though in the kitchen she was obviously able to rein that in. During the last round, Grace had noticed not only her intensity, but her air of acceptance, as though she was surrendering somehow to the ingredients. Following them instead of trying to lead. Grace wondered how she'd learned to achieve such a mature perspective. Maybe her dad's death forced her to grow up more quickly. As the balls flew toward her, she wondered if Yaz had healed, and added a few more memories to the universe.

Less than an hour later, so excited about her discovery at the docks that she couldn't hit one more ball, but still so unresolved about what she could or should say, she was back in the suite. Yaz's bedroom door was open, so she poked her head in. It was empty. Like, empty empty. No clothes. No balled-up towels or room service dishes. No Yaz. Her mouth tasted like sand. Back in the foyer, she noticed that the chocolates were still on the table, unopened, and the note she'd left was flipped over. *It now read: Mr. Barney came by to let you know a room opened up, but it was a single; I took it.*

Brutal.

CHAPTER THIRTEEN

Round Three, Day Four

"So, *that* was entertaining."

"Oh, you saw that, did you?" Grace had just walked out of the conference room studio after an embarrassingly honest post-cook-day interview. Lyn's observation was bang on. Detailing the litany of mistakes she'd made in the preparation of her goat cheese dish would make for great TV. Living with the consequences just plain sucked. She was mired in those thoughts when Lyn intercepted her.

"Yep. I saw it all. You did well. In the interview, I mean." Lyn smiled, walking along with her.

"I know what you meant." Grace was more abrupt than she'd meant to be.

Lyn stopped and grabbed her sleeve. "Are you okay, Gracie?"

"Nope. Not okay." She pulled away and kept walking. She didn't want to be rude, but she was tired. Mentally. Physically. She hadn't felt comfortable in the suite since Yaz moved out. Not that she'd felt comfortable in it before, thanks to her dad. "After listing the obvious problems, the judges said my dish was flat and unimaginative."

"I wasn't asking about your dish."

"Damn, Lyn, how am I supposed to feel?" She didn't even know the answer to that question. Embarrassed? Humiliated? Defeated? Deserted?

Lyn stepped in front of her, and Grace couldn't bring herself to look up, staring instead at her feet.

"Do you wanna talk about it?"

Out of the corner of her eye, Grace could see they were standing next to a small atrium with a sitting area. "Not really. Yes. No. I really don't know what's going on with me. I watched Kew and Yaz yesterday on set, that's how detached I was from my dish, and I could see them moving as if they were dancing with their ingredients. They were clearly in the flow and barely using their notes. I could see it, feel it, from my station. My performance, on the other hand, has been so inconsistent. So flawed. I don't think I've been in the flow in, well, forever. And on top of it all, my roommate couldn't move out quickly enough…"

"Hang on. Back it up." Lyn led her to a small settee. "Sit. Did you say *performance*?"

Grace heard the tone. *Uh-oh.* "Yes, I mean, technically my skills are there…"

"Sweetie, this isn't about skills. Cooking is not *performance*. It isn't tennis. You aren't served up a ball merely to return it over the net. Or to follow the recipes in a book. Your job as a chef, your gift, Gracie, is to accept the ingredients given and transform them. To add a bit of yourself to the dish. Otherwise we might as well leave it to AI to do the cooking for us."

"I…um…" Grace couldn't defend herself.

"You saw what Yaz did this week. Even with the penalty she'd been saddled with, she brought a bit of her heart, her family and her history, and she reimagined that goat cheese. Exalted it. That is not performance. That is…"

"Love. I know. Bette's favorite quote, right? Cooking is love made visible." She sighed. "Maybe I'm just not capable of putting my heart into anything."

"That's bullshit." Lyn could always be counted on for clarity. "Do I need to remind you about the cookies?"

The cookies. No. Grace didn't need reminding. She would never forget. She'd made cookies for Joss. Snickerdoodles. Her favorite. One of her last requests. Grace looked at a long stretch of windows that lined the hallway across from where she and Lyn sat. Rain slid down the glass, reflecting light from the opening above the atrium in short bursts, signaling breaks in the clouds. Petals from cherry blossoms had floated down from the trees like confetti, thrown by the swirling breeze against the windows, before riding gravity-compelled channels of water like tiny pink-and-white kayaks.

Lyn sat quietly and eventually Grace turned her attention to what she'd said. Joss Sanyal was not only Grace's first love, but she was also Lyn's only child. She and Grace had been inseparable from that first school dance until university, when Grace had been sent to a finance school in Zurich by her parents and Joss had chosen UBC, mostly for the ski team. She'd been an amazing skier, and during the pandemic had taken her online classes from her mom's chalet in Whistler. When they'd returned to Vancouver, they'd only just begun to settle back into each other when fate stepped in and decided that a long relationship was not in the cards for them, because a long life was not in the cards for Joss. She'd been heroic in her battle with the cancer, keeping a sense of humor that at times was dark. "I always wanted to go downhill fast," she had once quipped on receiving her prognosis.

In Joss's last days, Grace would not leave her side despite Bette's and Lyn's encouragement to take time for herself. Finally, Joss had begged her to go and bake her some snickerdoodles. At that time, she didn't know how to make much beyond toast and that was only because of her experience at the diner. But she'd taken up the challenge.

Grace managed a smile while fighting back tears. "Lyn, I burned the crap out of those cookies. I mean, they were scorched."

"True. But Joss loved them. She ate every single one. You know why?" At this point, Grace let her tears fall freely. "Because *you* made them. Because *you* put love into them. And *because* she loved you so much, those cookies tasted heavenly."

They sat quietly in their shared grief. Eventually, Grace spoke. "I don't have to tell you, Lyn, that none of what happened to Joss was fair."

"None of what happened to *us* was fair, Grace. It happened to *us*. And to everyone who loved her. But we're all better for having known her. Your cooking skills sure are!"

"Well, the Cordon Bleu helped."

"Not in the last round it didn't. Gracie, what happened?"

"No love, I guess." Grace thought about her dish. Her disconnect with the food. And with Yaz. "But I live to cook another day because my budgeting was on point." She laughed. "Seems like a sad consolation."

"Really? Hmm."

"What 'hmm'? The budgeting?" She knew what Lyn was saying without saying. It was what she always knew but, because she so stridently opposed her family's support in what they considered "the foundation of the business," would never admit. "Okay, I concede. I love numbers. I love budgeting and planning. And investing. And financing. I love it all. Numbers are tidy. And perfect. And constant." Grace took a breath and wiped her nose on her sleeve before accepting a tissue from Lyn. "Is that what you wanted to hear? I know my family sure does!"

Lyn put a hand on her shoulder. "Maybe I wanted *you* to hear it."

"Well, I'm aware. But I also love the hospitality industry. Love the people. Love the food. It's not…antiseptic, you know? Like sitting in an office all day. I just can't do that. As much as my folks want me to." Grace could feel emotion rising and needed an out. "In *spite* of what they want." She blew her nose.

"It's messy," Lyn said simply. "Cooking, I mean."

Grace put her elbows on her knees and held up her head. "Fuck."

"Yep."

"So how is it that the executive chef and owner of how many…? Five…restaurants is hanging out at her wife's workplace?"

"Are you asking me if I have somewhere else I need to be?" Lyn laughed and slapped her thigh. "How rude."

"Does Bette even know you're here?"

"Of course, she does. We have a room." Lyn winked and knocked Grace's elbow off her knee, forcing her to sit up. "But to answer your first question, I'm in the process of hiring a few new chefs. To replace me."

"Are you okay?" Grace immediately jumped to the worst scenario. "Are you sick?"

"Of course not, I'm fine. A bit bored, I'll admit. I think this is a normal part of moving into the next stage of restaurant ownership. I do get to retire someday, ya know! Until then, I want a bit more time to live." Lyn paused. "Speaking of life, since Joss died, you have been a bit like a boat in the middle of the ocean. Sure, you've changed your career, but let's face it, Gracie, you've otherwise thrown down an anchor and decided that you're staying put. Socially. Emotionally. Dare I say romantically? Being adrift was shitty for a while there, I get it, but you've swung a bit too far. That boat has become an island. For one. Which is not living at all."

"I had no choice. You know my family. I had to get away from them."

"That perfume you wear isn't about your family."

"What?" But she knew what. Her throat constricted again, and the tears returned. Her body spray's heavy vanilla, caramel, and cinnamon notes had a striking similarity to snickerdoodles. The perfume had been given to her by Joss before she'd died. Joss, who'd teased her that it reminded her of the cookies, "Except not burnt." *Dark humor indeed.*

Lyn took Grace's hand and turned her until they were facing each other. "When my precious daughter got sick, I couldn't help but think I'd done something somehow to cause it. Genetics maybe? Or something I'd fed her as a child. Or paint in her nursery. Plastic bottles. A million possibilities. It's normal to think that if only you'd done just one single thing differently, your loved one would be okay. I know you don't think the burnt cookies had anything to do with Joss dying…" she laughed, "though they could've been considered hazardous to anyone's health. Seriously. But the perfume. I know you wear it because it reminds you of Joss. You might believe that it keeps you in place, with her, alive. But love shouldn't anchor you, it should buoy you. And I think part of you is ready to let the heaviness go. It's time to come ashore, Gracie Donahue. And I think there's an even bigger part of you that already has a harbor in mind."

Grace gasped. *God, was it that obvious?*

"Yaz." She shook her head and closed her eyes. "She can't stand me. With good reason."

Grace filled Lyn in on the AWOL incident. "But she's so amazing, that even with the penalty she still had one of the round's best dishes. You know that in addition to her job at Lola's, she also volunteers at Safe Harbor?"

"I do. In fact, I know Sabrina Marline from way back. She was a talent then, and I've heard through the grapevine that her little setback earlier this week turned out well thanks to your friend's little intervention. Yaz has clearly benefitted from her tutelage."

"I'm not sure I stand a chance. God, that girl can cook."

"I've always felt that way about butch women!" Her eyebrows popped up and down cartoonishly.

"You have a filthy mind, Lyn."

"True."

"I really wish she believed me. I didn't rat her out."

"The optics suggest otherwise, but I do believe you. The truth will eventually come out."

Not soon enough. "I have a strong suspicion, though, who might've had a hand in it." She wanted to say more.

"But you don't know for sure, so can't say." Lyn knew her well. "Fortunately, the repercussions for Yaz were minimal, but let me see if I can find out how they might've found out that she'd left. I have an 'in' with one of the producers." Lyn gave her another ridiculous eyebrow pop as they pulled themselves off the little couch.

"Thanks. And thanks for the pep talk. There's a lot to take in, but I'll think about what you said."

"Grace, I've seen you cook with heart and no skills. And I've seen you cook with skills and no heart. All you must do is put the best together. Keep your heart open and the rest will follow."

CHAPTER FOURTEEN

Round Four, Day One

Yaz pulled herself off the bed and walked the eight steps to the door. As expected on "ingredient reveal day," it was Tiff.

"Jesus, Yaz, you really downsized."

"You nailed it there."

Her new "fair is fair" room was nice. At least okay. She could see part of the mountains over the harbor, but most of the view was of the parking lot and loading docks. There was a bed. And a small couch. Not like *the* couch. Nothing at all like *the* couch. To her surprise, it wasn't even that perfectly crafted, nap-inducing piece of furniture she missed most. It was Grace. She tried not to feel badly about ending things so abruptly. Grace had betrayed her. Lied. She'd almost gotten rid of Yaz from the competition but would have to settle for losing her as a roommate.

"So it's lamb for this round." Tiff looked up from her clipboard, probably not surprised to see what Yaz imagined was the expected reaction from contestants. Yaz would immediately look around the room for inspiration. She'd seen Grace do the same. Then, as ideas began to percolate, they'd usually smile and nod, energized by the possibilities they'd landed on for their dishes.

But today, Yaz had to dig deep for just the tiniest bit of enthusiasm. "Lamb," she repeated. Nothing more. It wasn't the ingredient that left her flat. She knew that as angry as she was, she was also disappointed. And disappointment was a completely different thing. And a surprise.

"Hey, I've been meaning to ask you, what were those little pink flowers you put on your dessert last round? And the ripple in it?"

"Oh, the gelato?" She realized she'd checked out of the conversation, and since it wasn't Tiff she was angry at, or disappointed in, or whatever this whole Grace mess was, she opted to pull herself together and make a better effort. Also, she was proud of her dish, managing to stretch the goat cheese and milk out as far as possible by making a cherry gelato. And also managing to avoid the distraction that was Grace Donahue. "The ripple was cajeta casera, kind of like dulce de leche but made with goat's milk. And I sprinkled it with sakura." Yaz checked to see if Tiff was still on board. Nope. "Sakura are pickled cherry blossom flowers, which I also used to make the gastrique…the little dots I put around the rim of the bowl."

She made a mental note to thank her mom for sending her the sakura. Or, if she won, to thank her in person.

"Well, it was pretty awesome, Yaz, and I heard the judges raving about it afterward," she said, handing her the tablet. "Gotta dash. See you in an hour!"

She plunked herself on the tiny hard couch and put her feet up on the tiny soulless coffee table. Nope, nothing like the suite. No sweetness. No cinnamon. No vanilla. No Grace.

Just lamb. Yaz knew that Salt Spring Island, in addition to being known for goat cheese, was also famous for its lamb.

Something she'd read recently by a local food blogger said that they feed on a crazy mix of salal, a blue antioxidant superstar, wild blackberries, and grapes. It seemed that this diet combined with the unique terroir of the area gave the lamb a special flavor, and since that was a feather in B.C.'s food hat, Yaz figured it was likely that tomorrow would involve another flight to the island.

Yaz surfed through several sites for ideas, then considered that her most successful dishes thus far had been Asian-inspired. Would it be playing into a stereotype to do another? Why not? Doing so would be completely true to herself. To her family of origin. Wasn't that what Grace was doing by ratting her out? Staying true to her family of origin? Damn it. Were there any thoughts Yaz could have without bringing the Donahues, one in particular, into it?

She rerouted her mental meandering. Lamb ribs, maybe with a barbecue sauce made with some white miso for earthiness, charred grapes, and Simps Peach Syrup, to draw out the inherent sweetness of the grilled meat. She'd come across the syrup while foraging in the studio pantry last round and had made a mental note to find a purpose for the Kelowna-made flavor-bomb. It was sweet. Like Grace with the pygmy goats. In a battle for cuteness between the two, there'd be no way to pick a winner.

Focus.

There were only six contestants remaining, and Yaz hadn't been impressed from a talent perspective with Kaley or Vij, despite how she liked them personally, or Brassard, despite his culinary lineage. Kew, on the other hand, was a wizard. And Grace, though technically sound and a whiz with budgets, hadn't yet excelled with the food. Moments of brilliance, yes, that was undeniable. She was, after all, picked to be on the show. But why was she even competing? She didn't need the money given the safety net she had stretched beneath her. Much as she protested, her family was doing everything possible to give her advantages. She'd land on her feet. On warm tiles courtesy of King-of-Hotels Daddy Donahue.

Yaz's dad came to mind. Before the bad deal that changed the Sano family's life, he'd also wanted the best for her. She was daddy's little girl, an expression that became a family joke when Yaz overtook him by more than a foot in height. But even so, she looked up to him. It was still hard to imagine how a failure in business could have taken him down such a very dark road. One that ended with his death. Any doubts she had about her own abilities, she realized, were trivial in comparison. She had survived another round in the competition. She had not let the injustices of the world take her down then, and she would not going forward. There was hope. And where there was hope, there was victory.

❖

Round Four, Day Three

"Grace, it's hard to believe the turnaround you've made after last week."

"Thank you, Chef Tremblay."

Grace had been worried when the first comment from the judges had to do with how her "budget continues to be an advantage," but it was followed by a series of raves not only about her technique, but about the perfection of her choices and the exquisite plating. She had Lyn to thank, because this round, she'd truly put her heart into her dish.

Each step she took with the tender protein was thoughtful. She used sweet aromatics like cinnamon and allspice to set up a Moroccan theme. She'd never visited the country, but *Casablanca* was her favorite film and it always struck her that there was little in it about North African cuisine. In fairness, Bogart's character owned Rick's American Café, so probably no surprise.

Grace had tied each ingredient to the other with intent. Ras el hanout candied almonds were strewn around the plate as a textural and decorative component. The judges were right. She *had* worked magic with numbers and was able to select a White Brut from Grey Monk Estate Winery in the Okanagan Valley to complete the film's iconic French 75 cocktail. The bubbly's notes of apricot could not complement the Moroccan dish more perfectly. Finally, her use of local sumac and early blackberries tied the dish to B.C. and gave the dish a tart counterpoint to the grilled cumin-crusted earthiness of the meat. Tart and earthy were inspired not so much by the film or either country, but by the chef who worked at the station beside hers. It had taken every bit of energy she had to maintain any kind of focus, given that Yaz was so close. She'd been a beautiful distraction. Efficient and fast. Magical with an astonishingly precise mise en place amidst the discarded pots and dishes. Yaz was elegant and athletic as she'd moved back and forth between station appliances. She was organized in the anarchy at a level beyond what Grace knew she was capable of.

But distractions aside, Grace had managed to do well. The single concern she had, as she walked back to the Stew 'n' Brew, was caused by the guest judge, David Marchant. He had credentials and was a celebrity restauranteur—her family had even patronized his restaurant—but then, as now, he seemed somehow *off*. His comments were complimentary, but he'd made her feel uncomfortable with lingering looks at her cleavage. He'd even licked his lips while his eyes made a meal of her legs. *Creep.*

Grace turned the final corridor in what they'd come to call "the rat maze." Her mood picked up as she spotted Yaz on her way to adjudication. "Good luck," she offered, wanting to reconnect and support. But rather than acknowledge the gesture, Yaz's eyes darkened, then went icy cold. The hallway temperature dropped several degrees. Yaz had every right to be angry, but not at her. Nonetheless, until there was more proof than a sightline from Brassard's room to the hotel back exit, it wasn't fair to share her suspicions. With any luck, Lyn would reach out with confirmation. The sooner the better, because she felt strangely lost in the large, mostly empty suite. She realized how Yaz had filled the space with a relaxed intensity. Not frenetic. Focused. It reminded her of how she prepared to receive a tennis serve. In the zone. But not tense. Determined. Yet insouciant. Grace wished that some of Yaz's temperament could rub off on her. The thought of Yaz rubbing anything on Grace stirred feelings wholly inappropriate in the wake of Chef McCreepy and were handily shut down. Hopefully, the truth would restore things, whatever those things were, between them. Maybe then Grace could further explore the fantasies she'd been entertaining about Yaz, the ones that caused her heart and other parts to pound so readily.

"Hey, Grace, how'd it go?" Kew handed her a grapefruit Bubly as she settled in for the agonizing wait.

"Not terribly, but did anyone pick up on a weird vibe from Chef Marchant?"

Kaley threw up her hand. "Honestly, I thought I was imagining it, but he seemed more interested in my, well, my boobs than in my dish."

"Exactly." Grace hadn't imagined it.

"Well, he wasn't interested in *my* boobs," laughed Brassard.

"Shut up, Christian," Kew and Vij said in unison, both in a way that made it clear there was to be no further commentary. Ever-petulant, Brassard went to the fridge for another beer and muttered something about how craft-brewed IPAs are overrated.

Kew invited Grace to sit beside him on the couch and quietly asked her if she was okay.

"Yes. I mean, it was uncomfortable in there, but most of the critique was good. You?"

"It's hard to go wrong with lamb, really. But otherwise, Grace? You seem a bit down, and I heard that Yaz found another room?"

Grace could see that Brassard had buried himself in a *People* magazine, and Vij and Kaley were playing cards, and she liked and trusted Kew so felt comfortable sharing.

"Yes. She did. For whatever reason, she thinks I had something to do with her being caught going AWOL." She shot a look at Brassard. "I didn't, but—"

The door to the room opened and Yaz walked in. Her head was down, and she was visibly shaking. All eyes were on her, but no one dared say a word. The room went quiet as she took a seat. When she lifted her head, Grace could see her face had lost all color. She immediately grabbed a bottle of water and walked it over to her.

"Yaz, are you okay?"

When Yaz wouldn't answer or accept the water, Grace set the bottle on the table in front of her. Not sure if she'd been heard, she tried again. "Yaz, are you—"

"Stay in your lane, Grace."
Ouch.

❖

Five years.
What are the odds?
Yaz hadn't laid eyes on David Marchant for five years. *Why now? Why here?* As she'd stood in front of the judges, she'd hoped he wouldn't remember her. Right, Yaz, like super-tall Japanese butch chefs were a dime a dozen. Hope died quickly. His criticism of her dish was completely out of line with the other judges' and although she'd managed to remain stoic, when he'd declared that her barbecue sauce was too tart, "like a lemon," she'd immediately recoiled. He'd nicknamed her Yuzu after the small sour citrus fruit because he'd told her when she'd worked for him that she puckered her face at him as if sucking on a lemon. He hadn't forgotten her. Not at all. Yuzu. The nickname was doubly insulting, because to call her Yuzu was not only personally and culturally derogative, and inaccurate, but unprofessional. If only that had been the only crude behavior she'd experienced. "It's my kitchen," he'd explained. That was true. And he'd used his position to berate her every chance he got. Her mirepoix was never diced small enough. The proteins were never cooked to his satisfaction. When she'd mounted the courage to ask if he had a problem with her, he'd claimed that he was "protecting his chance at a Michelin star." But of all the cooks in his kitchen, she'd been his only target. And now, even after five years since she quit, she was standing in front of him, her food being forked into his big fat mouth with his big fat hands, she was back in his kitchen. Pinned against the

freezer door. Those fat hands touching her. His fat mouth on her neck.

She wondered how long she'd been standing in front of the judges' table before her years of practice shutting out the shame kicked in. Jenni called it dissociative behavior, and she was right. Yaz had checked out. Her cousin was the only one she'd told about Marchant's assault, and when she'd refused to get support for the psychological aftermath, Jenni had taken it upon herself to read up on strategies that could help Yaz deal with it. Yaz didn't want to deal with it. She wanted to forget it.

"Compartmentalization can be useful if you need to accomplish a task and your emotions are getting in the way," Jenni had said. At the time, Yaz had plucked that tidbit out and for the most part ignored the sage advice that followed, advice that made it clear dissociative strategies were not necessarily good long term, "nor should they substitute for strategies of connection." Yaz wouldn't have remembered the whole of the strategy had it not been for the fact that Jenni was relentless about reminding her. "Yaz, you're already too quick to lock things away, to disengage. I love you too much to let you do that." It must've sunk in, because as those words materialized in front of her eyes now, she somehow found the strength to walk back into the studio with the other contestants for the judging summary. This time, she was able to stay in the moment. To her relief, in the end, the overall criticism must've been favorable because even with what she knew would be a dissenting vote cast her way from Chef Marchant, it was Kaley and Vij who were sent home. Again, she'd survived. She made a mental note to tell Jenni again how much she appreciated her not only as family, but as a best friend.

The bus ride back to the hotel was miserable. She was exhausted and fell back into silence. She could tell Grace kept trying to catch her eye, but she managed to avoid direct contact. People could be so disappointing. She felt numb. Lost in her thoughts. She would be able to avoid them all for at least a couple of days before the next round. Two to go. Four contestants left. All that mattered was right now. She had to get back into the present. Engage. And stay focused, or she would lose this opportunity. So, she refocused on the positives. Sabrina hadn't taken that drink. Her family, she knew, was cheering her on. And David Marchant hadn't managed, though he'd no doubt tried, to sink her chances at winning.

CHAPTER FIFTEEN

Round Five, Day Two

Grace had, like almost everyone who lived in or visited Vancouver, been to Stanley Park. She'd driven through it, biked around it, and hiked through it. One half offered views of English Bay and the Burrard Inlet, the other an impressive view of the Rocky Mountains making their ancient and rugged ascent from the West Vancouver coastline. Stanley Park was bomb. Grace had long felt it impossible to find a place on earth with a thicker forest of old growth Douglas fir and red cedar. Yet here she was. Right smack dab in the middle of one.

Surrounding her, gigantic reddish-brown trunks of ancient trees were stuck like birthday candles into a moss-green icing, and the sun bombarded the canopy with dapples and streams of light that made everything they bounced off more spectacular than anything she'd ever seen. *Beautiful* British Columbia, claimed its license plates. Underselling, Grace thought. It was *breathtaking*. This forest looked to her as fantastical as the one Tolkien must've imagined when he wrote *Lord of the Rings*. She wouldn't have been surprised to see gnomes, but that wasn't what she was searching for.

Today was all about the mushrooms, and the crew and contestants had been flown to Campbell River, then driven by jeep into a remote wilderness area. There, they'd been introduced to the hipster-trendy activity of gathering wild edible mushrooms by a master forager. Dakoeta Kinew had given a brief lesson on how to find and pick their target fungi in a manner that respected the land.

"I cannot stress enough," Dakoeta said, "that identifying spring fungi is paramount before anything is consumed. Many species that are edible look strikingly similar to those that are not. Some of these include ones that simply taste bad. Others, the ones you must respect, are highly toxic. Even deadly."

Grace could tell what was going through everyone's minds. Which was which? Anticipating the question, Perry stepped forward and put on her *listen carefully* voice.

"Identification is not a skill you will learn in one day, so in order to ensure your safety—and that of our judges—all of the mushrooms picked today will be vetted by Dakoeta's team of experts before being sent to the studio kitchens." Perry then did something Grace hadn't expected or imagined. She smiled and put her hand on the master forager's bicep and squeezed it familiarly.

Interesting.

"And as you may know," she continued both smiling and squeezing, "Dakoeta is one of B.C.'s foremost chefs, whose restaurant, Cougar in the Mist, is listed consistently as a top worldwide dining experience. Chef Kinew will be joining us on the judging panel tomorrow."

Each of them were given dull knives, a dust brush, and a basket marked with their name, Grace assumed so that whatever they picked would be what was on the correct cooking stations post-safety-check. By the time she'd picked up her equipment and map, Yaz had already migrated from the group. How was it possible that she'd still not been able to get her to look at her, let alone talk with her? And even if she had, what could she say. It wasn't fair to throw even someone as road-kill-worthy as Brassard under the proverbial bus until she had more than her own opinion. Since the judging last round, Yaz had been a ghost. And when she had appeared, she'd looked lost. Grace was starting to worry. No, she *was* worried.

"Come on, Grace," Kew said, "let's see what we can find."

She agreed, and Brassard followed behind. Her concerns for Yaz trumped her annoyance with him, so she didn't resist his presence as Kew led them into the woods. Beneath her feet was a thick carpet of ground cover that must be absorbing the sound, because everything seemed hushed.

Except, of course, for Brassard.

"My fraternity used to go foraging. Not as serious about mushrooms, maybe, as we were about getting sorority girls in the woods, but…"

"Christian. Please." Her generosity had lost patience.

"Sorry, Your Highness." He bowed.

Passive-aggressive asshole.

He continued, unfazed by Grace's scowl. "A lot of good 'shrooms grow in melt-off debris. I wonder if there are any magic ones growing around here. That would be awesome! I'm gonna go check near the creek bed." He then toddled off.

"Don't fall in." She couldn't have sounded less sincere.

Kew laughed. "I'm hoping to find some boletes. Or some oyster mushrooms."

"I'm sure whatever you find, you'll turn it into something delicious!"

"I hope that happens tomorrow. I could use the money to help with my dad's restaurant. He's a bit of a control freak, so there's no way I could work for him, but COVID was tough on his business."

Grace found herself wondering first about her own control freak dad, then about Yaz's father and his tragic business failing. There was more to that story, she could tell, but there was no way to know given how strained things had been between them.

"I sure wish I was better with budgeting," Kew said, helping Grace down an embankment. "I find it's the hardest part."

"Maybe you and I can trade places, or maybe just mix a bit of you and me in a petri dish to make a super-chef." She laughed, but also recognized in that moment that maybe in a very small way her family had done her a favor by footing the bill for her finance degree. The price, though? Too much. As she rolled her eyes, she caught a movement on a ridge above. Army green hiking pants. Blundstone boots. A red-and-black flannel shacket. Classic butch attire but perfectly fitting Yaz's lean frame. Her long legs traipsed easily over and through the deadfall. Quite simply, she wore it well.

"You like her, don't you?" Kew had followed Grace's sightline.

His comment surprised her a bit. She presented as high femme, had identified as straight before Joss, and now considered herself firmly in Camp Lesbian, singlehood notwithstanding. Few straight people had guessed at her choice. Certainly not many straight guys, given how many hit on her before turning away bewildered, or pissed. Maybe Brassard had tipped Kew off, though Kew seemed to share most everyone's disdain of the man-child. Or maybe whatever the feelings she was having for Yaz were closer to the surface than she'd been willing to admit. Strange given how difficult Yaz was to read, but there was something alluring about her, enough that Grace yearned to go carefully, page by page. If only she'd let her crack the cover.

"Good question, Kew. She obviously can't get far enough away from me, so how I feel might be pointless."

"Yeah, she was pretty clear about that in the Stew 'n' Brew. But she obviously wasn't herself. Something got under her skin. I'm sure you'll figure it out. My wife and I were like chalk and cheese at first. Besides, Yaz should be thrilled that going AWOL didn't sink her because now she gets to spend more time with you, her favorite target."

"Thanks, Kew." Grace laughed. "You're sweet."

Maybe once the truth came out about who ratted Yaz out, she'd be back to her old self. Grace missed her, but right now, she needed to stay in the game. "Hey, it looks like we're close to where the fire rolled through a couple of years ago. Didn't Dakoeta say that would be a good place to look?"

Dakoeta was right. Kew and Grace came back from the forest with their baskets full and handed them off to the foraging team. As they stepped onto the limo bus an hour later, Christian pushed his way past them so quickly that all Grace could see was his bloated red face with his hands pressed hard against his mouth. His speedy exit from the bus was followed by the sound of violent retching.

Several minutes later, as if to relieve a concern that might've been felt by those on the bus if Brassard hadn't been such a, well, Brassard, Chef Kinew stepped on board. "The fact that he's sick now is a good sign. More serious toxins usually take longer to show themselves," he explained. "I can't imagine why he would've eaten one without vetting, but we do have some remedies here for some of the more common toxins, and we'll make sure Christian is looked after."

This was the first time in days that Grace saw Yaz smile. *Thank you, forest.*

CHAPTER SIXTEEN

Round Five, Day Three

Yaz was as ready as she'd ever be but waited in the lobby until everyone had piled into the bus that was taking them to the studio for their cooking day. That would give her a choice of where she'd sit, and that choice would be as far from Grace as possible. It had been hard to keep so much distance from her, but she was beginning to process her feelings around the situation, and given that she'd made it through the last round, the edge was off the pain of the betrayal. As she stepped in and did a quick scan of the remaining seats, careful to avoid the penetrating glare from the back row, she noted that Brassard wasn't on board.

"Maybe he's already at the studio?" she heard someone say, followed by several other conjectures. "Did anyone see him at the hotel last night?" "This morning?" "I wonder what he ate." Funny, no one voiced hope that he was okay.

When she, Kew, and Grace were finished with makeup and back in the Stew 'n' Brew, they were joined by Tiff, Perry, and Bette. Perry claimed the center of the room.

"Today, it will be just the three of you in the studio kitchen," she declared, folding her arms.

"So Brassard is out?" Kew asked. "Like, permanently?"

"Maybe if he'd have shut up long enough to have heard what the forager said about eating without checking, he'd be here." It was clear Perry was angry. "Eating a cooked poisonous mushroom is bad, but eating it raw is even worse."

"Why is that?" Grace asked.

Perry turned to Tiff, who consulted her trusty clipboard. "Because humans have no enzymes to digest chitins," she read aloud, "which exist in raw and even undercooked mushrooms."

"And if he'd been listening," Perry stressed the word listening, "he might've heard Dakoeta—Chef Kinew— mention in his talk that the mushroom Christian was nibbling on like a mad squirrel, the one he thought was the pine mushroom, is not a spring grower. But its lookalike, the very poisonous amanita smithiana, is."

"Don't pine mushrooms smell like cinnamon?" Grace asked. "The poisonous ones don't give off that scent. I mean, he should've known, right?"

Yaz thought that Grace's comment was especially amusing, firstly because it sweetly but subtly put the onus directly on Brassard for his stupidity, and Yaz couldn't think of anyone more deserving. And secondly, Grace's observation about a pine mushroom's aroma made her smile because since day one, everything around her had smelled like cinnamon.

"Yes, that should've been a dead giveaway," said Bette, who quickly added, "No pun intended. Christian is not going to die. At least, not because of this folly."

What that "folly" would mean to the competition became Yaz's only concern. "But we're going to cook anyway?"

"You are. Christian is eliminated from this round forward, and the finale will include the three of you. Congratulations." Bette nodded at Grace, then at her and Kew.

"Your baskets have been checked, and your safe mushrooms are on your workstations," announced Tiff.

"Now is not the time to coast, people," Perry cautioned. "Just because you're advancing, this round will carry weight. Dishes will be scored and those tallies will be counted toward the final round."

"We'll call you when the crew is ready on set," Tiff added.

"Yaz, a word please?" Bette and Perry gestured to her to join them in the hallway.

Oh shit. What now?

Bette glanced around and spoke softly "So, we thought we'd have a chat with you about David Marchant."

Fuck. That.

Yaz stiffened, worried about where this conversation was headed.

"We, that is all of us including the regular judges, feel that his assessment of your lamb dish was quite simply unfounded," Perry stated.

"And unfair," Bette added. "His reputation, especially with female chefs, has since come into question, and we wanted you to be aware that he won't be asked back for future episodes. Ever."

I did not see that coming.

"Yaz, we tasted your food and agreed that it was delicious. It almost seemed like he was eating a totally different dish."

Yaz couldn't find the words to express anything beyond thanks. But inside, she felt that the universe had somehow righted itself. A karmic reckoning, maybe? She'd take it. As she returned to the Stew 'n' Brew to prepare her knives and review her notes, she felt lighter. Even the unwavering stare that resettled on her didn't feel as irritating as earlier in the day.

❖

Yaz's ease lasted only until they were called onto set, when she willingly gave rein back to her inner tiger. This was a competition, after all. She sprinted to her station and scanned her basket, pleased to see that virtually all her harvested mushrooms had been approved. Grace and Kew headed for the pantry to select their staples, and by the time she arrived only Grace remained. She was intently ferreting through the herbs, pulling out bunches of dill and parsley and adding them to armfuls already loaded with proteins and dairy selections. Yaz went for the spices and began to select from the list she'd created yesterday. Tarragon. What was Grace making, she wondered, suddenly aware of an odd sensation, like someone was staring at her. It had to be Grace, because it didn't feel like creepy prickles on the back of the neck, but more like a whole physical response, as if she was curled under a warm blanket on a cold winter night. She remembered her romance-obsessed cousin telling her once that there was a scientific basis to attraction, something about the body releasing chemicals, but that's not what this was. What was it? Nothing? Something?

"Tarragon?" Yaz said out loud, hoping to eliminate the distraction while struggling to find both the herb, and focus.

"Tarragon," Grace repeated as she reached into the herbs she'd just looked through and grabbed a bunch, handing it to her and walking off before Yaz could compose herself enough to thank her.

Right, okay. Back to it, Chef.

Dairy was next. Some spring Alpindon cheese, made in the province's Kootenay Valley, would pair perfectly with the oyster mushrooms she'd found yesterday growing on some decaying logs. It had a sharpness and some nutty notes and would also tie in with the asparagus she'd put on this round's wish list. Better safe than sorry. Everything she'd planned would be in harmony with spring and she lost herself in thoughts about what the judges might say. So lost, in fact, that when she turned to reach for some chicken breasts from the cooler behind her, she almost collided with Grace.

"Sorry," she managed.

"No, I'm sorry."

Like something out of a Chip 'n' Dale cartoon, they simultaneously turned in the same direction to avoid colliding and came perilously close to doing exactly that. Grace's ingredients began a slow surrender to gravity and momentum.

"Here, let me," Yaz said, taking a precariously perched bottle of chardonnay off Grace's load.

"Thanks."

Grace seemed surprised by her gesture, but like Yaz, probably realized that now was not the time for resolving their issue, nor to debate if that was even possible. For now, détente seemed fine. It was better than distraction. And warm blankets. For now. Wordlessly, they moved from each other's orbit. Yaz could already hear Kew banging pots around in the studio kitchen, so she picked up her pace. She hurriedly reached back into the poultry cooler and grabbed her protein, and when done foraging for the other necessities for her dish, returned and readied herself for the first of two of the most important preparations she would ever do. She could feel the butterflies in her stomach but ordered them to take a perch. The cook was on.

But the chef, it seemed, was off. Yaz realized as she emptied her bin on her cooking station's counter that it wasn't a package of chicken breasts she'd grabbed. Fuck. It was pheasant. Leaner than chicken. Similar flavor profile, but a touch earthier. Not the end of the world. No need to pounce. Just take a breath and think. Yaz organized her ingredients, her mind settling on a plan. She set about butchering the bird, with a plan to use the breasts and wings only. The wings would add fat to the breasts, and she would pay close attention as they pan-roasted to baste with herb butter as often as she could. Roasting the mushrooms would bring out the natural smokiness of the meat, too. Her mistake might end up being a "happy accident," as her mom liked to say. But it was also a reminder of the importance of focus.

CHAPTER SEVENTEEN

Round Six, Day Two-ish

Forty-eight hours later, just after eight a.m., the limo bus pulled away from the hotel. A push in the schedule had come about because the producers had decided that with just three contestants left, they could combine the schedules for the "reflection videos" and "ingredient reveal" into one day. They were also concerned, Tiff had explained to Yaz, that some spring rain was moving in later in the week, and the final procurement scenes were to be outdoor.

The pantry détente that began yesterday was still secure, mostly because Yaz realized that ultimately, it didn't matter who spotted her leaving. She was the one who left the hotel, knowing she was breaking the rules. Not that she wasn't still unsettled by Grace's broken promise. For some reason, that was sticking with her. Today, though, her sour mood had nothing to do with any of that. It was yesterday's mushroom round. Why did she have to blow up a challenge so late in the competition? Especially with an ingredient like mushrooms. She loved mushrooms. How could they have betrayed her? *Wait a sec.* Was she really blaming mushrooms? Was it possible she was misdirecting her anger? *Oh.* Was this a pattern? She gritted her teeth and felt her jaw clench. Okay, stand down, Yaz. Take a breath. It wasn't the mushrooms' fault. Mushrooms were intrinsically good, unless you were the one ingested by Brassard. Yaz almost smiled. And the dish she made with them was good. It really wasn't the mushrooms' fault. She blew air through puffed cheeks and shook her head. Her internal struggle must've been written on her face because Kew moved to the seat beside her and gave her a playful bump in the arm with his fist.

"Your dish was super solid, Yaz. It was just that fuckin' budgeting. I got lucky this time, but damn, I know how hard it is when there's a pantry full of so much good stuff. It's irresistible, especially when you want to make something spectacular. And you did."

From the back of the bus, a voice with all the sweetness of honey piped up. "Yes, Yaz, please don't forget that."

"Thanks," Yaz managed.

She found it inconceivable that Grace was still being nice to her. Until the conciliatory run-in as they'd gathered ingredients during the last round, she'd avoided all contact except when necessary. She'd thrown out the notes slipped under her hotel room door, without reading them. She'd even been overtly unkind. Not cool. She was still irritated with Grace. She was also irritated with herself for not being able to move past her anger completely. To forgive. Ultimately and even more irritating was the fact that Yaz couldn't stop thinking about the object of her probably misdirected wrath when she should be focused on the final round. Because third place didn't feel comfortable at all. That's where she figured she sat after the fifth round based on the judges' comments. Her mushroom dish was perfectly conceived and executed, they'd acknowledged, but her budgeting continued to be problematic. Pheasant and artisan cheese had tipped the scale away from her. That was the bottom line.

"You might have gotten away with one of those luxury ingredients, Yaz, but not both," Chef Kinew observed. "Delicious as they were, and in spite of how perfectly they highlighted the mushrooms."

Yaz cursed her younger self, the girl who railed against math because she could never imagine needing to calculate how high a kite was based on the string length and distance to the right angle. Not ever. Lesson learned too late because clearly, numbers were relevant after all. But no less a pain in her ass.

Kew struggled with budgeting too but came in just under the limit. It was only Grace who excelled at both deliverables in the last round. She put up an impressive spin on steak Diane, using a blue goat cheese from Agassiz, just an hour east of Vancouver, and a mixture of hedgehog, oyster, and cauliflower mushrooms that delivered, as one judge extolled, "the perfect mélange to entice every bit of flavor from the beef medallions." She was so smart to opt for an economical cut of meat. Going forward, Yaz would have to be especially mindful of costs. The star of tomorrow's dish would be salmon, and if she managed to catch a big one today, she'd have her kite flying at just the right height.

The drive to their fishing location was incredibly scenic, and while Kew and Grace chatted about mushrooms and salmon, hockey, and budgets, Yaz took in the picturesque drive along the north shore of the Fraser River. The mountains were verdant with spring growth, and only the odd small chunk of ice could be seen close to the shoreline. It was rare that the Fraser froze in modern day, but Yaz recalled just a few years ago having seen pictures on social media of an ice jam featuring thousands of frozen grizzly-bear-sized snow blocks strewn like a downed Jenga tower from shore to shore. Not this year, thank God, because ice-cold water was not in her wheelhouse. Any water, warm, cold, whatever, could not be above her knees. Non-swimmers had limits. Water was not her favorite element.

Yaz looked at Grace, struck as usual by eyes that flashed as she laughed along with whatever Kew was saying. Her thoughts flew through time to the moment on the couch when Grace was tending to her blister-burnt hand. Eyes locked on hers. Fingers touching her hair. Every one of her goose bumps betraying the effect Grace was having on her. She'd had trouble sleeping since that night, and it wasn't because the room downgrade featured a less than optimal mattress. It was as though a match had been lit. Grace's stroke of her palm had sent a bolt of heat through her, and every time she recalled the sizzle, which was far far too often, it was accompanied by a flash of what it might be like to have Grace touch her. Elsewhere. Everywhere. Despite her disdain for water, every thought of Grace made Yaz wet. *Now that's irony*. Her need for distance and her decision to keep a tight lid on her feelings were obviously at odds with the pressure building in the pot. Hopefully, she wouldn't have to put up with her much longer. There was only one challenge left, and it was for all the marbles.

After following the fork of the Harrison River for a bit, they were transferred to a small outboard motorboat and driven upstream for ten minutes or so until they arrived at the basecamp. The boats were pulled up onshore and they disembarked onto a pebbly shore. The crew had already set up the requisite equipment, which was minimal given that the sun was shining brightly on a small peninsula. Their location gave them an angle on action up and down stream. Yaz watched the slow steady flow of water as it rounded the spit, wondering how cold it was at this time of year.

"It looks icy-cold," Kew said, his tone hinting at a similar dread to what Yaz was feeling.

"Any chance the hot springs will have warmed it up?" Yaz had visited the popular hot springs along the south end of Lake Harrison several times and knew that it emptied into its namesake river not much farther upstream.

Kew laughed. "Doubt it. All of Harrison's water comes down from the Lillooet River. Like, a hundred and fifty miles north of here. Those hot springs don't stand a chance once they feed into Rocky Mountain water, Yaz. Glacial."

"So, cold?" She tried to sound serious but couldn't contain her smile. Kew nudged her, nearly toppling her over on the rocky riverbank. As she caught her balance, she stared deeper into the water below her feet. She was astonished by the speed at which the bubbles and debris raced beneath the deceptive calm of the surface, and immediately took several long steps inland.

"Good morning, chefs." Bette welcomed them, flanked by Perry, Tiff, and two people dressed like cover models for the *Canadian Stream* magazines she'd seen on her dentist's waiting room coffee table. "Congratulations on making it this far. Today will be your penultimate challenge. Catching salmon."

Perry got right down to business, as usual. "You'll be turned over to our hosts, Steve and Cheryl." She flourished her hand in front of the couple. "They'll give you a short lesson, and you'll then be outfitted with appropriate riverwear consisting of insulated neoprene hip waders, polarized sunglasses, a hat, a net, rod and reel, and a selection of flies."

"Are there really fish in this river?" Kew asked, intently scanning the water for signs of life.

"Indeed there are," Steve spoke assuredly. "At this time of year you'll find a few of the spring species, chinook, pink, sockeye, and if you're lucky, some spring coho."

Cheryl nudged Steve playfully aside. "You might even catch a steelhead, though that will have to be returned to the river since it is not part of your challenge. We make use of barbless hooks to ensure the safe return of any species that fall outside of the limits."

Yaz wasn't sure how she'd failed to appreciate what river fishing entailed, but it was only now grinding its way through her thick skull. "And will we have to actually go into the water to catch said fish?" Surely not.

"They're not going to come to you." Perry was obviously enjoying herself. "Any other questions, please ask our experts. The crews will be ready when you are."

❖

Well, this was different, Yaz thought as she trudged along the river's shoreline. Being in cold water up to her knees, but barely feeling it thanks to the insulated waders, was doable. Dealing with the rod, reel, fishing line, and net, that was the hard part. Grace and Kew seemed to take to it with greater confidence, and they'd already found spots upriver and put their lines in the water. It looked from a distance like Kew might've already caught one. The camera crews were with them, likely because not much was going to happen with her until she found a flat-bottomed and shallow spot to stand. Patience, isn't that what they say about fishing? *Take your time and watch your step, Tiger.* She could see a place just ahead of her where the water seemed calm, closer to the middle of the river, and was trying to avoid the deeper areas to get to it but wasn't ready to leave the shoreline. Just a step or two ahead was a small branch protruding from some rocks along the bank. She reached forward to grab it for extra support as she wove around a small pool that was protected from the flow by a collection of bowling-ball-sized stones just visible on the bottom. Left. Right. Left. Just as she was about to make her final step, her foot came down awkwardly on one of the stones. It flipped beneath her foot, and she rolled her ankle. *Fuck, that hurt!* Her knee buckled in response, and the top of the waders fell below the surface.

Instantly, cold water began to fill her right boot and the current pulled her leg into the pool. She grabbed the branch and scrambled to free her leg, but the weight of the water and the current that was pushing against it were too much. She tried to wriggle her foot out of the boot. Too tight. Her mind began to race, and she looked for more leverage along the shore, just feet from where she was mired.

Nothing.

Embarrassment at her predicament quickly gave way to the sense of panic that was building in her clenched gut. She was about to call for help from the crew upstream when her left knee went down, and that boot began to fill. The branch broke just then so now both legs were in the pool, filled with water that was tipping her forward in her boots. Without leverage and not wanting to take a header into the pool, Yaz let herself fall backwards into the shallower water behind her, downstream. *Fuck.* Ice-cold, Harrison-tributary-in-May water began to slosh up over her face. She gasped, then coughed as water filled her mouth. She spat it out, but the current was eager and unrelenting and it filled again. She struggled to get a breath, spewing and feeling a sense of nausea building in her gut.

Roll, Tiger.

She rolled, hoping that she'd regain purchase if her legs would roll along with her. They did not. Now she was facedown. *Not good!* She rolled again. *Yes!* She was freed from the pool, but the river wasn't ready to release her yet. Her body spun as the current pulled at her boots, dragging her downstream feet-first. Her back and sides were battered by river rocks that pushed the air out of her with every impact. She took every moment she could to find a breath in between the dips in the current.

One big surge swept over her, and she went under. Submerged, she scraped her hands along to bottom struggling to hold on to something that would stop her from being carried farther downstream. She could hear thunder. Maybe it was rocks, racking against each other like submerged billiard balls? Or was it voices? *God, let it be voices!* The Harrison heaved her up and slammed her ear against a rock on the way back down, causing her to scream. The scream filled her head, and the water began to fill her lungs. She felt a searing chest pain and saw only flashes of the sun through white bubbles. She could taste the minerally fluid as it forced its way up her nose and down her throat. Exhausted, Yaz could find no strategy except to surrender to the raging cold that rushed over and into her body.

❖

"Caught anything yet, Grace?" Kew asked from slightly farther upstream.

"Not yet," she whispered as loudly as she needed, knowing from every fishing experience she'd ever had—her father was an avid angler and had on occasion dragged the family out "to bond"—that fish liked quiet. She questioned now whether that was just something her dad said to keep her and her brother from chatting, since pretty much everything he'd ever done was far from altruistic. It—every action, plan, or purpose—had to serve him in some way, shape, or form.

Kew had already caught a keeper. A large spring coho. As she imagined the dish she'd be able to create with such a great catch, Grace felt her line go tight. She froze. Then the tip of her rod bent, signaling an almost indetectable tug. "Oh, I think I have a bite!" The cameramen moved closer, the boom swinging to catch her reaction.

She let a bit of line out, then pulled on the line sharply to set the hook. She began to reel up the slack and saw the fish breach the surface. The flash was silver. And huge. The camera crews drew away from Kew and moved closer, their boots splashing water across the narrow river and the microphone boom arching in her direction. The fish bolted like an old typewriter carriage return to the far shore, then zigzagged back, forcing the crew to keep out of range. She pulled the net from her belt hook and set it in front of her, alternately reeling and pulling the line toward her. Grace maintained a steady and quick pressure, not wanting to tire it out too much in case it fell outside regulations and had to be returned. Once she had it close enough to her, she dipped the net underneath its belly, and that's when she heard the scream.

Yaz!

She turned downstream, in the direction of the cry. No Yaz. Strange, last time she'd checked, just minutes ago, she was walking up the shoreline about fifty yards downriver. Then she saw the toe of a boot waving in the current. Then a hand. Her heart dropped and she quickly realized the perilous situation that Yaz was now in. *Get to her.*

Grace ran down the river in half the time it took her to carefully plod up it, her mind filled with worry and her heart filled with fear. She tripped only once, but it was close enough to Yaz's prone body that she was able to claw her way the final few yards. She reached under Yaz's head and pulled up from her collar, the weight of the soaked figure made heavier by the current. Yaz's face emerged, lips blue and eyes closed. Grace inserted her legs beneath the motionless torso to raise more of her up above the surface, then pulled with everything she had to couch Yaz in her arms and protect her from the current.

"Yaz? Yaz!" Grace's voice caught in her throat, the panic accelerating at the lack of response. She nudged a cheek and Yaz's head fell to the side. She felt her convulse before coughing and returning what seemed like half the river back into it. Grace took a breath along with her. "That's it, Yaz. You're okay."

Grace pulled her closer. She was shivering. They were both shivering. She noticed a watery red trail along Yaz's neck and followed it up to her ear. The gash was small, but she imagined it hurt like hell. "Medic! Medic!" she cried.

The crew was just seconds behind, and they descended en masse, lifting Yaz from her arms and pulling her out of the stream. Steve, a massive man who was clearly sure on his feet in the stream picked her up with surprising ease and carried her behind the crew to shore. One of the staff medics stepped toward her and directed her onto the bow of one of the beached boats. She strained to see where they'd taken Yaz when she noticed Bette walking toward her.

Tears filled her eyes, their warmth oddly comforting given that the rest of her was wet and freezing. "Where is she?"

Bette put a hand on Grace's shoulder as the medic wrapped her with an insulated silver blanket. "My guess is that she's already halfway to the landing, the way Cheryl was driving that outboard. The other medic is with them, and an ambulance will meet her there. Are you okay? What do you need?"

"I'm fine. I…" What *do* I need? Grace's first instinct was to jump in the beached boat she was sitting on and…and what? Race downstream after a woman who probably wouldn't have let her near her if she'd been more conscious? A woman who had sent up every stop sign known where she was concerned. Did what Grace need—whatever that was—really matter? "I'm good. I will be." She looked at Bette and her eyes filled. "I think the river isn't finished with me."

Bette pulled her closer and wrapped her with another blanket the medic had handed her. "Grace, she'll be okay. You need to be checked out." Bette nodded at the medic whose impatience and concern were obvious and stood to the side. "We'll head back as soon as we can."

All Grace had wanted, as she held Yaz in the river, was to see her brown eyes open. But all she could recall now was the blood, the mud, and the tiny pebbles of river rock that had coated and wedged into Yaz's soaked shirt. The gray pallor of her normally bright complexion. The way her wavy hair stuck to her head, streaked with red she now gathered was blood from the ear wound. *Yaz would be horrified. No flammable product.* She laughed, then a few more tears fell. "Bette, I thought she…I mean, she was breathing, right? She's okay, right?

"She will be. Now let the doc do her thing, and we'll get you back to the hotel."

❖

The suite felt bigger and quieter than ever. Grace walked to what had been Yaz's bedroom and leaned against the doorframe, wondering and worrying about what was going on. Bette had promised to keep her informed and she knew she would. But feelings of helplessness surrounded her, feelings not unlike those she'd experienced when Joss first got sick. Before diagnosis. Before the heart-shattering prognosis. Those feelings were like the river, flooding over Grace exactly where she had anchored herself. They drowned her belief that love was possible, and she knew that if she did not surrender, she would sink. Love? One-way maybe. Reciprocated? Not...

A knock at the door shook her out of her spiral. *Yaz?*

"Hi, Grace. You doing okay?" Bette and Lyn both stepped in, Lyn taking her into her arms and giving her a big squeeze.

"Yes. News on Yaz?" Grace pulled from the embrace with a quickness that said cut to the chase, please.

"I just got off the phone with Tiff, who is at the hospital now but about to head back with Yaz. She has been stitched up, pumped with some fluids, and is otherwise perfectly fine." Bette stared at Grace until they locked eyes. "She's fine," Bette repeated, nodding to make it doubly clear. "I've got a production meeting to go to. We've got some creative editing to get through, since things went not exactly according to script today." Bette smiled reassuringly. "But we're going ahead with the studio shoot tomorrow, so do what you can to get yourself back in the groove. And yes, we checked with Yaz and she is one-hundred percent on board with shooting the finale tomorrow. Nonetheless, given the situation, Perry has rescheduled the start time so everyone can have time for a relaxing dinner and a good night's sleep. Ten a.m. in the lobby. See you then."

"I can stay with you if you'd like," Lyn said.

"I think I'm okay." Grace forced a smile. "Thanks for letting me know."

"If you change your mind…"

"No, really, Lyn, I'm good. I love you guys."

She closed the door and once the bolt had been thrown, she pivoted and leaned against it, relief and anxiety weighing so heavily that she slid down to her butt and rested her forehead on her knees. She felt like she was being chased, and not just by the day's dramatic turn, or by the stress of the show. In fact, the stress had finally brought out the competitor in her. Lyn's talk had helped. Grace knew she was right about her being an island. Since Joss passed, five years ago, she hadn't truly dated, let alone opened herself up to so much as a one-night, no commitment affair. Not that she didn't have the itch. Or the opportunities. But she scratched that itch herself and intentionally avoided the non-battery-operated opportunities. Sex without love just wasn't interesting. Sex with someone she loved, now that was plenty interesting.

Yaz was interesting. A sexy butch, smart and driven. If it was possible, if Grace was right about the signals that had been firing between them, maybe she could at least let herself feel the attraction. Beyond the flirtation. Really feel it. But love? Could she let herself be loved? Because loving and being loved by Joss so deeply and then losing her nearly broke her. Even if she could pull free and float away from the fear that anchored her, then…then what? Hope that somehow, she could convince Yaz that she hadn't betrayed her? And did it matter? The only important thing was that she was okay. She'd been so gray. The blood. The blue lips. And just like that, the tears were back. Grace stayed in that position and cried until all her tears had fallen.

At dinner, she and Kew were both quieter than usual. He was a sweet guy, and obviously just as concerned about Yaz's welfare as she was. The sparse conversation gave her plenty of time to reengage mentally with the competition. She expected that the show, despite the day's drama would continue to follow the rules of the competition. That meant that neither she nor Yaz would have much salmon to work with. Who knew what happened with the fish she now barely remembered near-netting. Kew, on the other hand, had managed to catch a whopper so he would be fine, but they would both need to work miracles with the budget to give their limited portion of salmon a chance to impress the judges. No question they'd both put their effort into it, but until she could see for herself that Yaz was okay, her concentration was going to be an issue. It had gone the way of her fish. Into the deeps. Hopefully not like her chances of winning.

CHAPTER EIGHTEEN

Well, look what the cat dragged in!"
Lyn Sanyal crossed the hotel foyer with speed enough that Yaz couldn't escape the bear hug of an embrace even if she'd wanted to. She'd spent the afternoon being poked and prodded by a variety of hospital folks, and none of their touches elicited the warmth she was feeling in Lyn's arms. Especially not the stitches. Which reminded her…

"Ouch."

"Oh, I'm so sorry." Lyn stepped back, still holding her hands. "Did I hurt you? Oh, gosh, your head! Tiff said you needed stitches."

"Just two. And two more on my wrist."

Lyn released her hold as if Yaz's hand was on fire. "Oh, I am so sorry. Again. Are you okay?"

"I'm okay. Definitely happy to be back." She'd never been comfortable with being the center of attention, so she imagined that today was just about as uncomfortable as things could get. Her ankle still hurt from the initial twist, but maybe the cold from the river helped keep the swelling down. She remembered bits and pieces. The cold. Tumbling along the river bottom like human bedload. Clacking stones. For a moment, feeling strangely warm and safe. Not much else until she was being carted into the outboard and driven back to the launch. She wasn't sure if her injuries created more agony than the embarrassment.

"Come sit for a minute if you have the time. I'm sure you're anxious to get back to your room, but I have something to tell you and I'm sure Grace wouldn't mind."

Grace? *Oh, right.*

"We're not roommates anymore." Yaz wasn't sure what Lyn knew about the recent events.

"That's what I'd like to talk about."

Okay, I guess she knows it all. And apparently, Grace has no shortage of defenders. "Sure, I have a few minutes. The pain killers they gave me seem to be doing their job."

Lyn led Yaz to a small sitting area just off the lobby and they each took a seat facing each other.

"You know I'm Bette's partner, right?"

"Yes." *Strange start.*

"So I'm privy to some information about the goings-on in the competition. What I'm about to tell you, I hope, will remain between you, me, and Grace. Deal?"

Grace? Her track record on keeping secrets hadn't been great thus far, but whatever. "Okay, deal." Yaz had no idea what Lyn was alluding to.

"I know you think it was Grace who told the producers that you went off property last week."

True. "It's obvious that Grace would do pretty much anything to win. And I can't even imagine why she'd need to. I know about her family."

"If that's what you think, Yaz, then you know nothing." Lyn's tone was stern. "Come with me." She stood and crooked her finger at Yaz without looking back, and walked down the hall toward the hotel studio door

Fine.

Once inside, Lyn walked over to the lone production assistant who was obviously working on some tape and leaned over to say something that Yaz couldn't quite make out. She busied herself scanning the numerous monitors that showed different segments from the river shoot, frozen in time. There was Kew proudly displaying an insanely large salmon, his smile the only thing bigger than the fish. Various ambiance shots, like an osprey against the blue sky, the spring green tree line, and the river, filled all but one of the remaining monitors. Lyn tapped it with her finger. It was Grace. One hand was on her line, the other held the net. Her rod tip was bent dramatically. "That's the one. Can you give us a few minutes?"

The technician pointed to a switch and left the room.

"Sit," Lyn said, indicating the empty seat in front of the monitors and making it clear by her tone that it was not a request.

Fine.

"I'm not sure why you're predisposed to thinking the worst of Grace, and I'm sure you think you have good reason. Hopefully, you haven't made up your mind completely because that, Yaz, would be very disappointing. And sad." Lyn reached forward and hit a button on the keyboard.

Yaz watched as the screen showing Grace engaged. There was no sound associated with the video, so her focus was on the images that played out in front of her. The camera operator was standing downstream, and the shot angle was over Grace's shoulder. The shot zoomed in on her rod tip, which straightened and then bent even more as the line went taut. She was pulling on the line and reeling quickly. The camera panned to a flat surface of water several yards upriver. The river churned as a small fin cut through it. The fin grew and a large greenish-black fish emerged, arching up and then diving back below, sending up a splash of water as it did. The camera followed the line where it met the water for a couple of minutes, every now and then panning to Grace who continued to reel and pull the line. The rod tip dipped again, and Yaz was surprised it didn't break as the line pulled increasingly taut. The camera then set itself on Grace as she slid her net below where presumably the fish was. It was then that Grace's hand let go of the net completely and her body turned toward the camera. Her eyes were wide, stricken, and she appeared to be screaming. She took off downstream and the camera followed, zooming into the distance at a short span of rapids and what looked like a boot?

Fuck. My boot.

Then the camera frame widened so that the boot and Grace were now in the same shot downriver. The camera operator was clearly running along the shore, with branches blocking the scene and the shot angles bouncing up and down as they ran. Grace almost seemed like a cartoon character in a silent movie frantically splashing through knee-deep water, long legs kicking up the Harrison, every remaining bit of her fishing equipment jettisoned with each leap. She fell face first just short of the rapids, then crawled or floated, or both, toward the boot. *Toward me.*

The camera went behind trees again, and when it emerged, Grace's arms were wrapped around Yaz. The shot closed in on their faces. Grace was still screaming, looking desperately from Yaz, to the shore. Her eye makeup left dark streaks down her face, and eyes were liquid with worry.

Lyn hit a key and the tape stopped, the image frozen on the monitor. She put her hand on Yaz's shoulder. "Does this look like somebody who would do anything to win? You don't

know her, Yaz, and you'll never truly know her if you can't
see past this notion you seem to have that she is some sort of
precious spoiled princess."

Yaz's throat knotted.

"And by the way." Lyn sat down in the chair next to Yaz
and turned to face her. "It was Brassard who saw you leave
that day. It was Brassard who told Tiff. Not Gracie."

Not Grace?

Yaz bent her head and tried to swallow past the regret and
humiliation that were choking her. Lyn was right. Once again,
she had judged Grace and made assumptions about who she
was, that was true. It was wrong. Was there any way to set it
right?

"I'm so sorry," she croaked. "She's so…" Yaz wasn't sure
what she was going to say. Good? Beautiful? Lucky? "We're
so different. Her family…"

Lyn laughed. "Her family? The Donahues?" She laughed
again and shook her head. "You can't even begin to imagine
how intrusive those status-obsessed elitists are. How they
wouldn't let Gracie take summer jobs so that she'd have to
rely on them for college. How appearances are absolutely
everything to them. They would never acknowledge her
sexuality. Her choices. Ever." Lyn paused and took a breath.
Yaz noted that she was increasingly calling Grace Gracie.
There was genuine tenderness and love there. "You asked why
she would want to win? Because the Donahues—Gracie the
only notable exception—live their lives on a ledger sheet. And
on the social pages. Everything they *gave* Gracie growing up,
they expect to get back. And they're tenacious. Like hungry
dogs." Emotion began to choke Lyn's words.

Yaz sat quietly. She thought about her dad. How he'd been
up against some hungry dogs, and how they'd eaten him up.

How she couldn't save him from what followed. Tears began to fall.

Lyn pulled a tissue from a box on a nearby soundboard and handed it to Yaz. "Speaking of debts to be paid, some people might say you owe Gracie an apology. Those same people might also suggest that you have more in common than you might think."

"I doubt an apology would go very far." Yaz sighed. "I've said some mean things." *And thought many more.*

"I'm willing to bet that Gracie would be able to look past that. I've seen the way you two look at each other."

Yaz shifted in her seat. She knew she'd been looking. But Grace? "What do you mean?"

Lyn laughed. "Good lord, girl, it's shocking that neither of you have chopped your fingers off given how often you look at each other's stations during your cooking segments."

"What are you…"

"Don't believe me? The crew has wagers on every round. Will Grace look at Yaz more than Yaz looks at Grace? Honestly, you two are oblivious." Lyn threw her head back and laughed.

Yaz took a moment, thoughts flying around in her head like fireflies over a June meadow. When the truth began to settle, she corralled the few words she could manage. "I'm not sure we're compatible."

Lyn lifted her chin with one hand and patted her on the shoulder with the other, looked her square in the eyes, and declared, "That's what people said about jalapeños and blueberries, but guess what? They make one hell of a jam."

CHAPTER NINETEEN

Yaz stood to the side of the penthouse door, leaning partly on a single crutch, the other having been parked on the hallway's textured wallpaper. She wondered if eleven o'clock was too late to knock. She wondered too exactly what she was going to say, though since her chat with Lyn a million words had crossed her mind. Sorry being the most prevalent. She could wait until morning, but tomorrow was the finale. If she was going to focus on the competition, she needed to do this tonight. And she felt confident that Grace would benefit from hearing her out. She'd been more than patient with Yaz, and ultimately, Lyn was right. She owed her an apology.

It wasn't just the late hour that troubled her. What if Grace didn't want to talk? Maybe she'd pushed too hard. Maybe there was no room for forgiveness. And yet…the look on Grace's face, frozen on the monitor, said otherwise. "The way you two look at each other," was that what Lyn had said? She couldn't ignore her feelings. The water had washed away so much, including denial.

In the hours since, Yaz had come to understand that a strange thing had happened in the river. An unprecedented thing. For the first time ever, time slowed enough that she'd been able to feel only what *she* was feeling. She hadn't been thinking about her mom. Or her dad. Or Sabrina. Or the clients at the shelter. And she hadn't been internalizing other people's judgment or curiosity. She'd felt that way on so many occasions. Under a microscope. She knew it came from looking different. From being different. Being a tall Japanese woman meant she felt conspicuous both at home in Canada and when she visited Japan as a young woman. Add to that her identity as a masc-presenting lesbian. She was proud, yes, and her appearance had never caused an overt problem. She'd been stared at, sure. But beyond the ignorance and violence of Brassard and Marchant, she had never been bullied. Or bashed. Still, at times all she wanted was to blend into the masses. To go with the flow.

In the river, her only thought had been her own survival. The water rushed but time slowed. She couldn't remember a moment when she'd been so singularly focused on herself. It was oddly freeing. Not that she'd ever felt burdened by her responsibilities. Or embarrassed by who she was. But as she was pulled under, she was also free. It was crazy and ironic, she realized, that she'd given herself permission to live her life at the same moment as the river threatened to take it. Her own life. Just Yaz. And now she'd been given the chance. The time. Time to set things right. She owed it to herself. And to Grace.

She turned to the door and straightened her shirt, then pushed her hair back, careful to avoid the gauze patch behind her ear. She looked down at her feet and realized she was only wearing socks because the swelling in her bruised ankle made footwear impossible. It wasn't broken, thank God, and she could weight bear with only moderate pain, but she hoped that if she gave it a rest tonight, she might be able to avoid using the crutch tomorrow. First, though, she needed to stand up in a different way. She took a deep breath and slowly exhaled.

The door opened after the second knock and before she could say any one of those million words she'd rehearsed, Grace wrapped her into an embrace. Just as quickly, she let Yaz go and pulled her into the suite. Once the door was shut, Grace stepped back and wordlessly surveyed her from head to toe, not only with her eyes. She also lightly touched her near the bandage on her head, then trailed her fingers down to the wrap on her wrist, finally taking her free hand gently in hers and leading her into the living room.

"You're looking much better than when I last saw you." Grace smiled, then winced. "Are you okay?"

"I am, yes. Honestly." *Better now. Hello, couch, my old friend.* "The crutch is for show."

Grace set her crutch against the end of the couch and sat on the coffee table in front of her. Then, as if rethinking the decision, joined her on the couch but sat sideways with one leg bent beneath her so that she faced her. She leaned forward and put her palms on Yaz's cheeks, taking a moment to push back the unruly hair as it fell forward.

"Are you, really?"

"Well, I've been better." *And less aroused. Jeez, Yaz, calm down. You're here to apologize.* She gently took hold of Grace's wrists and lowered them, placing her hands palm down on her thighs. *Better.*

Grace reacted as though she'd crossed a line, leaning back a bit and respecting Yaz's space. She looked concerned and relieved at the same time; her brow furrowed but her smile was soft. It was then that Yaz realized Grace was in her pajamas. Soft cornflower satin complemented Grace perfectly, impossibly brightening the blue of her eyes and providing a perfect landing spot for the blond curls that fell lightly on her shoulders. Fine lace trimmed the bottom of the shorts, and the collar. L.L.Bean meets Victoria's Secret, heavy on the Secret. The effect the sleepwear was having on Yaz would doubtless keep her up all night.

"Oh, I'm so sorry, you were in bed? Heading to bed? It's late, Grace, and this can wait…" Yaz reached for the crutch and tried, somewhat half-heartedly, to push herself out of the couch. *Chicken.*

"God, don't be silly, Yaz. Sit down." Grace grabbed the crutch and put it out of her reach. "It's fine. We have a late start tomorrow. So technically, it's early. Now, what's the 'this'? Are you really okay?"

"I am. I will be." Yaz was surprised she'd been let in the door, given how poorly she'd been treating Grace. "Listen, I need to tell you something. Please."

Grace must've picked up on Yaz's earnestness because her brow furrow deepened, and her smile faded. "Go on."

"Do you remember me telling you about my dad?"

Grace looked surprised but nodded. "Of course I do. Fentanyl. Very sad, Yaz. I'm so sorry."

"Thanks. I'm not going to use him as an excuse, but the legacy of his situation has contributed to a mistrust I have. Of people who *have* advantages. Of people who *take* advantage. My dad's business failing came about because he trusted investors. And those investors reneged on a deal."

"They took advantage."

Yaz pushed through the emotions that were sticking in her throat. "More than that, they stole from him. From our family. He couldn't bear it. And I think I may have gone a bit overboard as a result, suspecting that you were dishonest because of who you are," Yaz recalled what Lyn had told her about the Donahues and corrected herself, "that is, who your *family* is. I am sorry. Truly sorry. It wasn't fair, or right, and I can't apologize to you enough."

Grace nodded. "I appreciate the start, Yaz. And you were partly right, about people who have it all and take advantage. It turns out it was Brassard." She said it matter-of-factly.

"How did *you* find out?"

"I suspected. I went down to the loading dock, to see if there was a camera, and I saw him standing in a window just above it."

"Why didn't you tell me?"

"I didn't know for sure. Lots of people have rooms that overlook the docks. I left notes under your door trying to explain my suspicions…"

Yaz winced. "The notes. I, uh…I couldn't read them, Grace. Well, I could've, but I didn't."

"It's okay, I get it. I didn't want to wrongly accuse anyone."

"Like I did." The truth landed with a thud in Yaz's chest.

"Tiff only confirmed Brassard's involvement today." Grace smiled. "I think she felt sorry for me."

"Why?"

"I was a bit of a mess on the bus this afternoon. Coming back from the river. Without you."

"You clean up well." Yaz managed a smile and put a hand on Grace's.

Grace turned her hand and entwined her fingers with hers. She leaned forward and touched Yaz's lips. "Your lips were so blue, Yaz. I was so scared. I don't know what would've happened if you'd…well, you are okay, right?"

"Other than having difficulty concentrating?" Yaz swallowed and waited for Grace's fingers to lower. Was she flirting? Or was this just concern? The river incident would have terrified anybody, right? She looked deeply into Grace's eyes, so deeply that she wanted to ease her mind and convince her that she was more than okay. In her company, she was awesome. Instead, she looked away, afraid that she was misinterpreting Grace's kindness. Maybe it was the pain meds that were making her heartbeat quicken. And softening the edges around Grace's tousled blond hair. "So why did Brassard have such a hate-on for you?"

"I went on a date with a friend of his. A guy not so different from him."

Yaz mustered up every bit of self-control to keep Grace from seeing her instant reaction. She could easily have shown her one, because an unexpected surge of jealousy pounded in her gut, but she had no right. People could be with whomever they wanted. Even men. The envy was quickly replaced with disappointment, surprising Yaz with its depth. She realized that Grace was staring at her, and she felt a flush of embarrassment.

"It wasn't really a date, per se," Grace explained. "I was his plus-one."

In less than ten seconds, Yaz's emotional roller coaster had zipped by jealousy, disappointment, embarrassment, and had pulled into the station of relief. "Like, for a wedding?"

"Yes. My tennis partner's. He was a groomsman, and he had no date, so I agreed to accompany him as a favor to her." Grace turned Yaz's palm up and ran her finger along the now healed rope burn on the unbandaged wrist, then bent down and kissed it.

Flirting? Check. Yaz thought she was going to explode with the yearning she was feeling. She felt as hot as the river had been cold, and worried that if she opened her mouth every word in the English language even remotely describing how intensely aroused she was would come pouring out with a force that would put the waters of the Harrison to shame.

"Oh." *Or not. Maybe it was the meds.*

"What can I say, Yaz. It was a crazy time. I'd just lost Joss and Grannie Jean just two months prior. I felt it all piled on. My decision-making was compromised. Obvs."

"Of course. Grace, I'm not throwing shade. I might be a bit surprised."

Yaz smiled and released Grace's hand, then moved hers behind Grace's back, gently pulling her closer until their bodies were only inches apart. "But it ended?" Yaz teased her, lightening the moment. "With Brassard's friend?"

Yaz's leg jumped at the swift and strong squeeze of Grace's hand above her knee. This was followed by another involuntary reaction when Grace's fingers slowly traced the seam of her jeans until they molded against a spot mid-thigh. That spot immediately caught fire. And that fire accelerated like a meteor until it collided with a wet spot—a very wet spot—that did nothing to diminish its intensity. Nothing. She looked in Grace's eyes and the fire raged. How was that possible? Grace must've noticed the question mark that creased her brow because she tilted her head and again tried to explain. *Not about the fire. Or the wet spot. Or how naked she was in Yaz's fire-addled mind.*

"I was his 'plus-one.' He was all dressed up, but he was no gentleman. And yes, it ended."

Yaz felt Grace's hand behind her neck, fingers tickling the hair on her nape. She shuddered as she was pulled closer, so close that she could feel the heat flash in what could only have been two inches between them. "Badly?"

Grace nodded and smiled coyly, playing along, fingers more persistent against the back of Yaz's head. "Yes, my dear Yaz, it ended quite badly actually, for a variety of reasons, not the least of which is this."

The remaining distance disappeared as their lips met. The kiss started gently, but as Yaz melted further into the couch and Grace melted into her, it quickly became a mutual demand. They claimed each other's lips, surrendered their mouths, and opened themselves to each other. Tongues wrapped around each other, probed deeply, pulling moans from depths that Yaz had never imagined.

"Did I hurt you?" Grace asked.

"No, not at all. Impossible." *Liar*. "Okay, maybe just a tiny bit. The head."

Yaz moved Grace's hand from near the bandaged and stitched gash behind her ear and put it on her shoulder. *Better*. Then she kissed her in a way that could leave no doubt what her intentions were, teasing out Grace's bottom lip and then releasing it and running her tongue along the top. Grace responded in perfect kind.

Yaz pulled back and waited until Grace opened her eyes before asking, "Is this a good idea?"

"Kissing is always a good idea, Yaz."

"And what if I'd like to do more than just kiss you?" As if to demonstrate, she began slowly unfastening the top button of Grace's satin blues. Grace inhaled sharply, her nipples clearly straining beneath the flimsy fabric.

"I'm not sure what you have in mind, though I have a few ideas of my own." Yaz felt Grace's fingers graze her nipples through her shirt. Then Grace leaned in to nibble on her earlobe before whispering, "I guess I'd want to know if whatever we do tonight," she paused and licked the earlobe, "will change the way we cook tomorrow?"

Yaz gasped as Grace gently bit her neck. Pleasure rolled across her body, goose bumps like river rocks stirred by a torrent of longing, and she immersed herself in the exquisite sensation until she could find words. "I think if we do it right, it'll change everything about tomorrow."

❖

"Promise you'll tell me if something hurts?"

"That's usually my line." Yaz winked and wove her fingers through Grace's hair, exposing her neck and ear before claiming them both with her mouth.

"You're such a butch," she groaned, knowing by the small gush between her legs that Yaz had discovered a particularly erogenous spot. When she could find her breath, she opened her eyes and pulled back so that she could explore Yaz's eyes. "I especially like that about you. Don't forget that for the future." She punctuated the demand with a tug on Yaz's shirt. "But tonight, given your, er, physical challenges, would you allow me to take a firm lead with what is about to happen?" She intentionally stressed the word firm, which caused Yaz to shift beneath her, producing another small gush of pleasure where she straddled.

"I can only try, Grace, but you are making me crazy and if something goes awry, I could plead temporary insanity."

She smiled and tugged Yaz's shirt from her jeans, then undid each button without taking her eyes off her. "If that's the case, I think I can do something to get you off." With that, she ran her hands up Yaz's ribs and took each wonderfully hardened nipple between her fingers through the tight cotton tank top and squeezed. Yaz bucked and arched, the ensuing moan captured by Grace's mouth.

Grace was encouraged by the response and though topping was not her forte, she'd certainly had a few fantasies about Yaz and this might be the time to live them out. After all, it was clear by Yaz's usually controlled demeanor that she enjoyed taking the lead. Grace looked forward to that, and even the notion of being under Yaz increased her heart rate. But tonight she was going to make sure Yaz was comfortably pleasured. "Let me know if something we're doing hurts, please? I'll go slowly."

Yaz rolled her eyes. "Not too slowly, I hope." Already her voice began to scrape with sexual tension.

Grace squeezed her nipples as a reminder that she was going to look after things this time. "Patience, Yaz, I'd like to learn your body and that will take as long as it takes."

She pulled Yaz forward by the lapels of her now unbuttoned shirt and leaned into her. She freed the shirt and tossed it over her shoulder before pushing her back into the couch. That's when she saw the tiger. The glimpse of the tattoo she'd seen when treating Yaz's rope burn now stared fully back at her. Ending with the tail at her wrist, the cat was depicted in a stalking position, its hind legs taking up the lower arm to just above the elbow, the torso filling in her upper arm, and the upper haunches and neck hugging her shoulder. Now, with Yaz half-undressed, the predator looked like it had ducked beneath the black tank's shoulder strap, its head emerging on her upper pectoral muscle, below her clavicle. The jet-black eyes were intent on prey, somewhere out of sight but near where her nipple was visible, taut beneath the fabric. The tiger's teeth were bared and a pink tongue dripped with glistening saliva. The artwork was perfection, the colors vibrant, the lines precise. The subject reflected the same intensity that the wearer possessed. She slowly ran her fingers along each beautiful inch, delighted with the goose bumps that followed beneath her touch. When she'd finished petting the beautiful beast, she slipped her hands under the tank barely able to resist gasping at the tightly carved muscles beneath. Grace's nipples hardened and she pressed more deeply into Yaz, her hands squeezing between the supple couch and the hard body to pull her closer. Even seated, Grace felt her curves fit perfectly into the inviting angles of Yaz's body. She squeezed her thighs against Yaz's and claimed her lips, slipping her tongue deeply into the yielding mouth beneath. As she did, Yaz's hands moved up her thighs, and thumbs began to circle near her center, moving the fabric of her shorts so that they tightened between her folds. She was slick and wanted to be touched but needed to stave off her desire until she'd pleasured Yaz. She leaned back and pulled the hands from below, careful to avoid the wrist bandage. "Unbutton my top," she managed, hearing the raw desire in her own voice.

Yaz complied, but slowly. Grace was enjoying the unfamiliar assertiveness, taking in Yaz's obvious delight as the satin was pushed back over her shoulders. She leaned forward and let Yaz take each breast into her hands and then each nipple between her lips, while she lifted the tank top between sucks and pulled it over her head, gently so that the injured ear was spared contact. They kissed as Grace reached down between them to unbutton Yaz's jeans, her pelvis grinding against the top of her thighs, before she slid onto the floor and spread Yaz's legs. "Take them off, or I will."

Within seconds, Yaz had complied and her jeans and boxers were thrown aside, all while watching Grace touch her own nipples. She loved the look on Yaz's face, eyes unquestioningly riveted on her body, yet simultaneously aware of the pleasure coursing through her own. And then there was her own pleasure. Grace was not disappointed. Naked except for the two white gauze patches, Yaz was a specimen. Long, lean, and muscled, her chest almost smooth except for the wonderfully erect nipples. A small, trimmed tuft of hair marked where her thighs came together. It was all Grace could do to keep calm in front of the handsome beauty before her. Her hunger grew.

"You are so gorgeous, Yaz. I need to taste you." She leaned back on her heels and spread Yaz's legs in front of her. Her scent was intoxicating, and her mound glistened. Grace eased her hands between and beneath her thighs, pushing down on the couch cushion until her palms could lift Yaz's butt, but not so far that her thumbs weren't free to explore the dripping folds. She circled the edges of the clit and Yaz responded by raising her arms over the back of the couch and using the leverage to move up and down against the gentle pressure.

Grace was soon aware that crouched as she was, her satin shorts had pulled tighter between her mound, and as she moved forward to taste Yaz, a small spark of ecstasy shot into her belly. She shouldered Yaz's knees and swirled her tongue in the wetness where her thumbs had been, the dance marked by changes in pressure and rhythm, each choreographed by Yaz's moans and movements. Legs against her back pulled her closer and deeper. The satin strained alongside her own throbbing clit, and the wetness there surprised her. She draped her tongue along the length of Yaz's clit, enjoying the hard heat, and then circling it slowly until she heard her breath catch and a small tremor shook her inner thighs. She slowed, knowing how close Yaz was but not ready for the song to end. With each stroke of her tongue, she moved around the delicious dance floor of Yaz's sex, rocking forward and back in rhythm with Yaz's lifts and descents on the couch. As the time between strokes and sparks shortened, the dance between them grew ferociously stronger, penetrated more deeply. The beat pounded and their bodies responded. Grace felt Yaz take a handful of her hair and pull her more deeply into her, and she obliged by moving a thumb into her, pressing upward to stimulate the spongy ledge within. She marveled as Yaz's butt began to tighten in Grace's hands, and her thighs shook against the sides of her neck. Her heart was pounding wildly, wetness between her legs flowing in pulses that were becoming longer waves, and she knew her own orgasm was about to shatter any remaining resolve. She plunged deeper and took Yaz wholly into her mouth, sucking her clit and dancing on satin until they both broke wide open.

When the waves leveled out and the music faded into the background, Grace slid upward and curled against Yaz, who'd all but been absorbed by the couch. She pushed back the maverick strand from her forehead and stroked her cheek gently. "You are so delicious, Yaz Sano."

Yaz cupped Grace's chin and kissed her. "And that was…" her voice was ragged and trailed off, her body still vibrating with aftershocks.

"Yes, yes it really was."

CHAPTER TWENTY

Round Six, The Finale

The Stew 'n' Brew had a very different vibe on the morning of the finale. The usual conversations about the ingredient of the day had been replaced with quiet contemplation and a nervous energy that had Yaz's leg bouncing up and down, Grace tapping her pencil on her notepad, and Kew pulling relentlessly at an apron thread.

Yaz wondered if she'd ever be able to focus after what had gone on between her and Grace the night before. Before heading down to the lobby this morning, they had discussed the importance of the day, and how they both owed it to themselves and each other to put their dramatically revised status on hold. That was the idea. The reality of this pact was much harder. Every time she looked at Grace she had flashes of her doing things that brought her nipples to attention and a wet heat to her core. But it was impossible not to look. Grace was quite simply beautiful. Naturally beautiful. Her full lips seemed even fuller this morning. Her cute nose even cuter. The lake blue eyes even bluer. Grace's pencil stilled and it was only then that Yaz realized she was staring back. Heat brushed her cheeks, and her breath hitched.

"Are you two trying to make today easier on me?" Kew laughed. "Because I'll take it."

His comment landed with a humor that sprung the tension from them all, and they had just a moment to settle before Tiff walked into the room to announce that they were ready on set. They'd drawn straws this round to see who would go out first, not that it really mattered, but they all agreed they wanted it to be fair.

"Good luck," Kew said as he headed out. "Let's show 'em what we've got!"

Yaz gathered her notes. She was second to start and Tiff had just waved her toward the stage. Just before reaching the door, Grace tugged on her sleeve, and she stopped in her tracks. Grace leaned in and kissed her cheek, then whispered in her ear, "It's game time, Sano, and I'm coming for you." Emphasis on coming. Yaz almost melted in her boots.

❖

As Grace unpacked her knives and began setting up her mise en place, her mind drifted to the night before. The taste of Yaz on her tongue, the feel of her flesh as it writhed beneath her hands, the rhythm of their movement, the clenching of her fingers, and the arch of her back as Yaz had released. And then her own release, how she'd fallen forward into Yaz's lap, her cheek on the still-trembling thighs, the perfume of sated desire filling her head. She felt herself flush and warm with the memories and wondered as she looked across the studio how Yaz was able to stand up. Her own legs felt like wet noodles and she hadn't been the one who'd almost drowned the day before. But Yaz had slept soundly, eventually, and had awakened in good shape. The swelling of her ankle was half of what it was so she could at least wear shoes. Grace could see that she was already immersed in her prep, working with her usual focus and intensity.

She wanted to honor the pledge she and Yaz had made this morning, about staying focused and making the dish of a lifetime, so she began to trim the salmon she'd been afforded. Yes, it was minimal, but it was chinook and its flesh was prized for its buttery flavor. She sliced it thinly and laid it on top of some edible flower petals she'd strewn on fresh circular rice paper. The soft pillowy base reminded her of Yaz's cheek, and her lips tingled. She wondered what fabulous concoction Yaz was going to create, and involuntarily looked across the studio only to find attention fixed on her. This was not going to be easy. At all. She did her best to look admonishingly at Yaz until she looked back down at her station, then returned to her prep. Maitake mushrooms were sending up an aroma from her sauté pan that was musky yet sweet. Again, Yaz crossed her mind. Rather than fight the distraction, she decided to embrace it. After all, it had been the most satisfying night and if it at all influenced her dish, the sensuality could only make it better. Cook with your heart, she smiled to herself, and other parts as needed.

Once the mushrooms were ready, she pureed them into a deep rich stock, strained it, and filled three small cappuccino cups with the dark brown liquid. On top, she spooned a shrimp foam that mimicked a milk froth. Eventually, she pulled herself and her ingredients together in a way that brought her joy. It was the first time she'd ever experienced the sensation while cooking. Something had shifted. The mushroom shrimp cup was placed on each of the judge's plates beside the wrapped and steamed salmon. The colorful petals were visible beneath the translucent rice paper, intentionally mimicking the goat cheese rounds from Salt Spring, especially once she'd artfully fanned several crab crisps around the edges of the plates. It was a dish comprised of savory ingredients, but it appeared sweet and whimsical, like something enjoyed at a modern bakery café. She had conceived it as an ode to Vancouver's coffee culture but realized, as she admired its beauty, that it was inspired by Yaz. It was love made visible.

❖

The swelling in Yaz's ankle had subsided, but the long walks from stove to fridge to pantry made the pain more noticeable as the studio session went on. She attributed her endurance to a physicality the night before that had an unexpectedly energizing effect. Maybe because she'd fallen into an almost embarrassingly solid sleep immediately after her earth-shattering orgasm. Yaz was unaccustomed to being quite so passive during sex, and it had felt even more un-butch-like not to have reciprocated, but she felt confident that there would be opportunities to return the pleasures. Fortunately, Grace had brought about her own climax, marked by a satisfied moan and quiver that just by proxy almost drove Yaz to another of her own.

The ankle and the memories were doing nothing to help her with her dish. Neither was watching Grace across the studio kitchen. Yaz was typically efficient in the kitchen, and Grace with perhaps two exceptions seemed almost chronically organized, as if her recipe was a prescription. Today, though, a different Grace had shown up. No measuring of this or that, no precise temperature gauges in sight, no tiny tweezers placing tiny garnishes around pristine plates. This Grace appeared to be responding instinctively, organically, to the ingredients.

Yaz watched her move with an easy confidence at her station. Grace was in the zone. Yaz focused in on her lips as she tasted a sauce, her plump luscious mouth and pink sexy-as-hell tongue the very best kind of distraction. Since arriving at the studio, she'd looked for an opportunity to touch her. Kiss her. But it was the finale and cameras were everywhere. They'd agreed there was no reason to make things public, though they'd discussed how unsurprised most people in their circle would be if they did get caught in a moment. Now, those same cameras seemed focused on Grace. *Can't blame them. If I were a camera, I'd be on Grace too.* As if on cue, an always-genuine smile brightened Grace's entire visage as she checked on some maitake she was sauteing. Yaz could smell them from across the kitchen, and their intoxicating earthy quality pushed her right back into memories of the night before. Grace caught her looking and with a single stern look, twinkling regardless, reminded Yaz of their agreement. Focus on your dish.

With not much salmon to work with, Yaz decided to stick with tradition. Her own B.C.-Japanese tradition. Inspired by Chef Hidekazu Tojo's groundbreaking B.C. roll, a local favorite comprised of cucumber and BBQ salmon in an otherwise traditional sushi rice and nori, Yaz decided to take a similar gamble. And it was a gamble. Sushi purists would consider anything outside of classical washoku ingredients as culinary heresy. But a nod to local fare seemed more acceptable to modern diners and fit with the goal of the show. She felt the risk would pay off.

By the time the clock signaled an end to the final dish, she had created something beyond the usual. As she took her plate to the judges' table, she also took great pride. It was an impressive salmon maki made with local wild Ojibwe rice and a maple-syrup compressed striped rhubarb wrap in place of the seaweed. The drizzle for the unique roll was made with kaki, a Japanese persimmon her mom had provided, with cinnamon and vanilla back notes. *Snickerdoodles.* Nothing about the roll was usual. And nothing was without intent. Today had been a good day.

❖

Yaz, Grace, and Kew stood in front of the judges' panel, holding hands for both moral support and to keep themselves from collapsing from sheer exhaustion. This was it. The finale. In minutes they would know the results. Grace took it all in. The lights and cameras. The crew members who seemed equally excited and nervous about the results. Perry, Bette, Tiff, and Lyn stood to the side, smiles and pride written on their faces. The judges' faces, on the other hand, were unreadable. Like poker players, except looking to give away the pot rather than win it themselves. A squeeze of her hand by Yaz reeled her back in as the first judge, Carolyn Conceptione, began to speak. She looked at Yaz, and Grace felt the squeeze tighten.

"Yaz Sano. You cook creatively, showcasing the rich culture of Japan, a historically entrenched part of British Columbia's broad and cherished diaspora. Technically flawless, you produced dishes that never fell short of unique and delicious. On several occasions, you failed to respect the budgeting challenges. As you work your way up the ranks in this industry, and we fully expect you will, these skills will come to you as easily as your astonishing cooking does."

Grace felt Yaz's hand relax, and she leaned into her as Marcus Perrin addressed Kew.

"Yip Kew Leung. Throughout the competition you cooked impressive dishes, including today's seared salmon with spot prawn, asparagus and morel risotto. Most of the time you were within the budget allowance. However, especially in the final two challenges, your dishes fell just short of a bar that was raised exceptionally high by your two competitors."

Kew tipped his head in silent acknowledgement. Grace gave him a supportive nod and squeezed his hand. Then the final judge, Eleanor Tremblay, turned her attention to her. She put most of her energy into keeping her knees from buckling but knew that Yaz would not let her fall. Her mouth was dry, her heart pounding, as she awaited her adjudication.

"Grace Donahue. Culinarily, you were off to a rough start in this competition. However, you showed continued improvement and particularly in the last two rounds elevated your dishes to beyond what the judges had imagined with the ingredients you had. Moreover, in a world of rising food prices, something that weighs heavily on the average British Columbian, you proved that the gift of this province's exceptional bounty can be pushed to excellence while remaining on budget."

Chef Tremblay paused and looked at all three of them. "The winner of *Recipe for Success, Season Two*, is…"

CHAPTER TWENTY-ONE

Who won?"

"Who won?! Are you serious? How could you not know?"

Yaz sat up higher in the bed and shrugged. "I don't know, Grace, I was kind of occupied at the time. As if you didn't notice!"

It took less than a second for Grace to pull herself on top of Yaz and pin her to the mattress. She sunk lower, defenseless against the pleasurable onslaught and marveled at the wonderful way their bodies fit together. Grace was curvy, her hips and butt suitably muscled from her sport. Most nights and several mornings since the conclusion of *Recipe for Success*, Yaz had explored every delicious hill and valley, finding unimaginable beauty and excitement in each. Instinctively, she surrendered to her, slowly caressing the impossibly soft skin of her lower back as she gazed up into the deep blues. Grace's eyes were scrunched up in that way that said "I should be angry with you for not knowing," while also confessing they weren't entirely committed to it. It only took a second for her heart-stopping smile to break through as she propped up on an elbow and play-punched Yaz. "Seriously?"

"Not that it really matters, Grace, but I'm curious. Who won?"

Grace blew out an impatient breath and tucked a wavy lock of hair behind her ear, giving her a clear view into Yaz's eyes, likely to assure herself that Yaz was honestly in the dark. *She totally was.*

"The Canucks. They took it to game seven, then won in a second overtime period." Grace paused, scrunching up her eyes as if looking for evidence that Yaz already knew the Stanley Cup result. *She did not.*

Grace shook her head with obvious disbelief and continued. "Vancouver went completely mental. Street parties. A parade. Did you not notice the fireworks? Honestly, if I hadn't spent the last four months in your orbit, I'd wonder if you lived under a rock." She squeezed her shoulders, then leaned down and kissed her cheek. "You're very cute when you're oblivious."

Yaz felt the way she always felt when Grace was near. Connected. Present. And always a bit excited. She was a beautiful woman in so many ways, and their relationship was by far the best thing to come out of the competition.

"Oh my God. The competition. The show." Yaz felt herself panicking. "What time is it?"

"Relax, baby, we have time. We asked everyone to come around eight. It's barely four." Grace eased herself off Yaz, pulled on a T-shirt she'd freed from the twisted bedding, and disappeared into the walk-in closet. "The finale doesn't air until nine. We're good."

Time had taken on new qualities in the past few months. Since the river incident, Yaz had changed, or at least her perspective had. She'd always felt like time was being stolen from her, feeding her impulsivity and temper, but she'd come to realize that the loss was at her own hand. She'd chosen to waste time on anger. Anger toward her dad, for his choice to leave her and her mom. Anger at everyone who made her feel like a victim. Even at Grace, for perceived wrongs. The river changed that. She'd been shown herself: judging others, holding grudges, protecting her heart from harm. Since then, she'd taken a huge emotional step forward on so many fronts, realizing that her father was more than his addiction. After all, she wasn't expected to fix his choices. Her mom had tried to no avail, and Yaz was a teenager at the time he peaked in his addiction. What could she do? Not everything, it occurred to her, was absolute, especially when it came to the people we love. Her only job was to love her dad. Not fix him. Or revise history. Understanding that allowed her to replace the pain with memories of the best side of him. While she worked on profoundly altering the legacy of her dad in her heart, Grace was taking steps to do the same with her parents. She wasn't in a place where she wanted them in her close circle, but she'd told them about the competition, and they'd seemed excited to watch. They'd met Yaz, and it was only slightly awkward, or as Grace optimistically remarked afterward, "for the Donahues, that was progress."

Yaz also decided, as she adjusted to life with Grace, that to love was to risk, and that in time, harm could and would heal. She loved Grace and knew in her heart that Grace loved her. Time had given her gifts and going forward she was going to treasure them.

"Yaz? Remember, when I asked if you needed help unpacking some of your stuff?"

Grace's query lifted her from her ruminations, and though Yaz detected no hint of admonishment, she mentally scolded herself. After all, it had been three months since they'd moved in together and she still hadn't emptied all the dozen or so boxes she'd brought to their new place. Grace had turned over a new leaf when it came to daily living and had already organized and probably categorized her clothes and shoes by some fashion standard Yaz knew nothing, happily, about. "Yes, babe, I promise I'll get to that tomorrow." Time had been both her enemy and her friend. She'd been back at her job at Lola's, worked her usual shifts at the shelter, and had spent what was left with Grace working on the next phase of things. Great things. Lots of great things. And multiple other, great things. Yaz smiled.

Grace's voice from the closet pulled her back. "No, sweetie, I know you've been busy, and again, there's no rush. In fact…I was going through a box just now looking for a pair of your boxers, and I found these."

Yaz turned toward the door as Grace emerged. The T-shirt Grace had just thrown on was gone and she stood in the doorway completely naked, perched on a pair of pink satin stilettos. It was all Yaz could do to take her eyes from Grace's beautiful body to the article she dangled from her hand. Yes, they were in fact boxers, but not a typical pair. This pair had a hole that accommodated a dildo. Grace had stuck a finger through it and was waggling it suggestively. Yaz felt a wave of excitement crash through her body, landing with an almost audible thump in her clenched and moist center.

"And since there's no rush at all…maybe you can model these for me while you explain how it is that these haven't factored into our playtimes thus far?"

Yaz almost jumped out of the bed to catch the harness briefs that Grace had tossed toward her. "Oh, uh, yes. I mean, er, nothing we've done has left me wanting." True, completely true. Yaz sat still on the edge of the bed, boxers in hand but nonetheless uncertain about how Grace felt. "And I wasn't sure, well…they're not everybody's cup of tea." Did she really say that out loud? Cup of tea? Gaaa. She could feel her face blazing, from embarrassment and excitement. She fell back onto the bed, feet still on the floor. Goose bumps rolled across her body.

"Sit up, Tiger." Grace's command was gentle yet insistent.

Grace stood directly in front of her, so close that Yaz could smell her sex. The strap-on was one of her personal favorite toys, but she hadn't found the courage to bring it to their bed. And she wasn't lying when she said that their sex life was entirely fulfilling. Grace must've sensed her internal debate, because a gentle finger pulled up on her chin until full attention was on her.

"Nothing AT ALL has left me wanting either, my darling. And thanks for being the best kind of gentle butch. I love your fingers, and I love your tongue. I love you, Yaz Sano, but as a chef you shouldn't need to be reminded that variety is the spice of life. And it so happens that this is a cup of tea I'd love to indulge in. Because I love you. So it's very, very okay to put this on and show me how you want to fuck me." Grace punctuated her suggestion by squeezing each of Yaz's nipples until she relented. Willingly.

Grace reached into the bedside table drawer and rummaged through until she found a dildo with a suitable base which she handed to Yaz. She then passed her a small egg vibrator and chased it with a deep and sexy kiss that almost vaulted Yaz off the edge of the bed. It quickly became clear to her that the strap-on equipment was not new to Grace, and Yaz's anxiety lessened as her excitement spiked. Once the dildo was in place, Yaz carefully inserted the small stimulator into a small wearer-side sleeve in the boxers. She wanted to keep Grace's pleasure at the front of her mind instead of on her own satisfaction, so would keep it switched off for now. There was so much she wanted to do, and as soon as she was set, she pulled Grace into her and took her mouth with hers. She put her hands in Grace's hair and pulled back gently but with enough force that Grace gasped. "Your word for stop is B.C. Do you understand?"

Grace moaned, then sighed an agreement. Yaz kissed her neck before positioning her gently onto the bed on all fours and sliding beneath her. One look at the pink stilettos on the white cotton sheets and Yaz could feel her heartrate skyrocket. *Thank you, Mr. Lou-whoever.*

Yaz pulled Grace's hips so that she was straddling her just above her waist. Grace brought her mouth down to hers, eagerly setting her breasts in Yaz's upturned palms. Hard nipples slipped between her fingers, and she squeezed, gently at first, then harder until Grace pulled away from the kiss and gasped. She could feel Grace's juices warm against her belly and felt her move so that the dildo inched closer to her opening.

"Not quite yet, Princess." Effortlessly, Yaz reached beneath Grace and lifted her up and toward the head of the bed. Grace took hold of the top of the headboard, which in fact was a railing that separated their loft bedroom from the rest of the apartment below. Yaz could see that she'd positioned herself so that her arms were hugging the rails and she was holding her own breasts, thumbs flicking and pressing into the taut nipples.

Yaz's head was flanked by Grace's knees, her slick folds spread above her mouth. Stilettos pressed against her hips, and she lingered, deeply breathing in the sensations that coaxed a tidal wave of raw lust from her core. Only then did she pull gently down on Grace's thighs to give her tongue access to the glossy, satiny center. With her tongue, she explored the outside edges, savoring the musky sweetness. Slowly, she began to move against Grace's rhythm, meeting the long easy rocks and feeling Grace deepen further into her as the movements quickened. Yaz knew that Grace was close to letting go. She wasn't ready to let her.

Yaz pulled Grace's hips and repositioned them near her own. Grace looked down at her, and without words and with a gaze never wavering from Yaz's, she slowly enveloped the dildo. Her eyelids fluttered and her breaths became ragged, deeper and then more even as she began to move with Yaz inside her. Yaz steadied her, fingers entwined, and elbows bent against the mattress to provide leverage. Grace moved with an easy rhythm, taking her tip to the edge of her opening, then sliding until Yaz was fully immersed. The small egg hit gently on her clit with each stroke and her own desires began to demand release. Grace released a hand and grabbed the headboard, adding speed and intensity to their hips' rising and falling. Her breath and moans filled the loft, echoing pure pleasure. *Not yet. Time. We have time.*

Yaz slowed Grace's hips and began to pull herself slowly out from under her. She felt Grace's resistance, and heard a gasp edged with disappointment. "Stay where you are," she said, her voice gravelly with desire. She moved several pillows below Grace's torso, and she relaxed into them. Yaz's heart filled with the trust she was being shown, and she was emboldened by it. "Put your hands here," she reached over Grace, and tapped the rails of the headboard. She pulled back the long waves of blond and fought the urge to nibble on the perfect ear. Instead, she whispered into it, "You can stop any time."

"I trust you, Tiger."

Yaz slid down Grace's back. She moved her fingers down Grace's spine, around her hips and down the back of her thighs. Yaz kissed the goose bumps left in their wake, feeling Grace's anticipation on her lips. She stroked her calves before slowly removing each pink shoe and tossing them aside. She then positioned herself so that the dildo was pressed against and between Grace's butt cheeks. She immersed her fingers in Grace's folds, her thumb teasing her clit ever so gently as she pressed more deeply. She shifted so that the tip of the dildo fell low enough for her to place it near Grace's wet sex, then adjusted so that her thighs fit against the back of Grace's. She pulled back slightly, then leaned into Grace. She reached around Grace's hips as she began to move forward, and felt Grace tilt her pelvis to accommodate entry into her dripping satiny vagina.

Slowly. There was time. "Go at your own pace, baby," Yaz whispered. "I'm in no rush."

"You feel good," Grace said, her back curving to bring her butt higher against Yaz. "That's it, Tiger. Yes. Oh God, that's perfect."

Yaz pressed forward again, then rocked back, filling Grace with each push. "Touch yourself," she said, and Grace obliged, wedging her hand between the pillow and her belly.

"Oh God," she purred. "So good."

Yaz managed to keep her stroke rhythmic, loving the exquisite sensation of each thrust against her groin, but soon became aware of the egg. Its vibration was still off but it had shifted between her folds, and she could feel it through the boxer fabric each time Grace's muscled, beautiful ass pushed into her. The distraction was impossible to ignore, and she felt her breath quicken, her strokes becoming longer and harder as she sought release.

Her brain was screaming for her to slow down. *Slow down. Take your time.*

A switch flipped in her head, and she pulled the pillow out from under Grace, carefully releasing the dildo. Before Grace could register the sudden disconnect, Yaz had flipped her on her back, spread her legs, and filled her again. Grace's legs wrapped around Yaz's lower back, her arms pulling their bodies so close it wouldn't have been possible for a feather to fit between them. Yaz gripped the headboard rails and began to push and pull, their bodies grinding, each movement sending swarms of pleasure to her core. "Is this okay?"

"Yes, Tiger, yes. Perfect. Fuck me."

Yaz felt Grace pull her in more deeply until they were both so wet that their juices had soaked through the boxers, a sensation that gave Yaz an extra boost of energy. Grace's darkened eyes began to flutter, and soon her moans became shorter and higher pitched. She was clearly desperate for release. Yaz was just barely aware of her own primal grunts, feeling as though their climaxes were stampeding toward them like wild horses. Yaz's hips registered a thrust as Grace bucked and arched, pushing even more deeply into her core. *It was time.* When they hit, an explosive orgasm was met immediately by another. *Grace's.* These were followed by a wondrous barrage of light and pulses of heat that moved through her body and between them. The sensations pushed them off the cliff together, until they fell into each other in a tangled heap of sweat and sheets and skin.

CHAPTER TWENTY-TWO

A couple of hours and one extra-long hot shower later, Yaz and Grace prepared to welcome their friends for the final televised episode of *Recipe for Success*. Jenni was the first to arrive—as was always the case for Yaz's fomo-forward cousin—and was greeted with hugs and smiles from them both. Yaz had been privy to conversations about fashion over the past couple of months between the two of them that might as well have been spoken in another language. Phrases like fringed and beaded maxi dresses, nineties redux, and slingback heels were bandied about with an obviously mutual understanding between Jenni and Grace and the more time the two of them had spent together over the last few months, the more their own friendship had grown. It warmed her heart.

Grace took the small wooden crate marked Penn Coves from under Jenni's arm and walked to the back of the large room and through a swinging door, while Jenni took in the space. After a thorough inspection, she surprised Yaz with a solid punch to the arm.

"It's about time you invited me to your new place! You've had a whole month to decorate, though, so I'm not sure why things are so sparse, unless minimalist is the look you're going for."

It was true. Aside from the TV, the couch, several chairs, coffee and side tables, the room was unadorned. The ceiling was high, the walls an antiqued barnboard, the floors wide-planked rustic wood. Large multi-paned windows started from the waist height and rose up ten feet or so. These covered the full walls on either side of the corner entryway. It reminded Yaz of the kind of space that would have been occupied by a pharmacy or corner store back in the sixties, and it was suitably located in a residential neighborhood next to a large park. Now, though, the building had been redesigned with another business in mind.

"It's a weird space to live in, but I think it has a good vibe," Jenni added. "And a good 'hood. Established. Quaint. I like it."

"I'll show you upstairs later. We've been focused up there since we moved in."

"I'm sure you have been!" Jenni laughed and gave Yaz another tap on the arm. "Where's Okaasan?"

"Mom went for a walk around the sea wall."

"Jeez, she never stops, does she?"

"I think she's happy that Auntie Miyuki is well enough to be on her own for a few months. She also told me she needs to work off the chocolate buffet."

Jenni's eyes flashed. "You put her up at the Sutton?" She looked as though she'd just finished the last turn of a Rubik's Cube. "That seals it. You won, Yaz! Didn't you? I knew it!"

"Whoa, cousin. I did not say that. For the millionth time since the filming wrapped up, I am under a strict non-disclosure agreement and cannot confirm or deny any…"

"Come on, Yaz! Just tell me!"

Yaz slowly took her phone out of her pocket and glanced at the screen. "You'll know in less than two hours, along with everyone else. Where's Emily?"

"She'll be here soon. Grace has her making a pie delivery to some fancy caterer up near Squamish."

"I'm glad Grace kept her on after graduation. And it must be nice to have a new roomie."

"And a friend. Who actually likes to shop." Jenni then looked up and down at Yaz, taking in her modest but, she felt, adequately boyish fashion choices.

"Speaking of roomies, how's Oyster?"

Jenni scowled. "Mr. Mashumaro, and yes, that is his name though you refuse to use it, is fine, thanks. He doesn't miss you a bit. Sleeps on your fave chair now. Craving oysters, are you?"

Yaz loved that her habit of calling Jenni's cat by her food whims caused her cousin distress. It was all in good fun, though she was loath to call any animal Mr. Mashumaro, despite how suited it was to the enormously puffy white cat.

"I saw the crate. What variety did you manage to find this early in the season?"

"Kusshis. Beach rolled and meaty as hell. So good."

The Kusshi variety of Pacific oyster was one of Yaz's favorites, and as she thought about the oceanic saltiness, she found herself thinking about Grace. How sweet she tasted. She recalled hearing someone say that eating an oyster was like kissing a mermaid and wondered where exactly that proverbial kiss was landing.

"Speaking of cat," Jenni asked. "What's with this look?" She wavy-pointed at Yaz's face, and tilted her head as if trying to figure out the puzzle.

"What look?"

"This cat-who-swallowed-the-canary look."

Yaz felt the heat rise from neck to forehead with the speed of the mercury in a candy thermometer.

Jenni was unrelenting. "And now the cat has got your tongue! Okay, I won't keep tormenting you about Grace, and how much you looooove her." Another arm tap punctuated the tease.

Jenni wasn't wrong. The months that passed since *Recipe for Success* wrapped up had changed her life. Their lives. And so much more was about to change.

"Alright, you two, let's get the food out before our guests arrive!"

"Grace, Yaz just told me who won!"

Grace stopped in her tracks and glanced at Yaz, who dropped her jaw, furrowed her brow, and shook her head emphatically, enough to communicate wordlessly the truth of Jenni's nearly successful ruse. "Jenni." She smiled. "Your cousin and I are both winners."

With that, Jenni rolled her eyes, fake-gagged, and walked to the door to let in the evening's first arrivals.

❖

"How did she miss it?" Grace laughed and threw her head back.

Yaz leaned into her. "I keep telling you, I was busy. And I'm not a hockey fan."

Jenni reached across the couch and delivered another tap on Yaz's arm. "I know, Grace, I keep telling her to get out more often. Read a newsfeed or check out Twitter. Does she? No, she doesn't."

"Don't hit my baby," Yaz's mom cautioned from her window seat near the TV. "You'll unleash the tiger!"

"I'd like to sic our tiger on that Brassard guy. I still can't believe he stole Grace's agar-agar and hid it at his station. Little jerk! He didn't even use it. It's like he took it just to spite you!" Jenni was outraged, but Grace just laughed it off.

"We've seen competitors do worse things," Bette admitted. "You'd be surprised. Fortunately, Grace's sweet pea and prawn panna-cotta-turned-île-flottante was genius."

"It all worked out, though, in so many ways." Grace beamed at Yaz, who again felt that tingle go through her the way she always did. The way she always hoped she would.

Everyone at the viewing party joined in the merriment, but Yaz's focus was on tonight's episode of *Recipe for Success*. It had been four months since the competition finale was filmed. She had no idea that the editing and production processes were so time-consuming and keeping the secret of who won had been killing her. Jenni was unremitting in trying to get her to spill, but everyone else like Sabrina and her mom, even Grace's Let 'Em Meat Pie assistant Emily, respected the non-disclosure rules that they had to follow. It was hard to keep the secret, but Yaz could see that on the television, the judges were delivering their final summaries of the dishes. It wouldn't be long. It was a night full of surprises, and she couldn't wait for the next big reveal.

Grace made a round of the small gathering with some smoked salmon lollipops as everyone settled in for the announcement.

"My God, Grace, these are ridiculously good." Lyn winked as she popped one into Bette's mouth.

"Shhh." Sabrina raised a lollipop presumably as a call for silence. "They're about to announce…" A drumroll echoed through the cavernous room, quieter now that everyone, including Yaz, was holding their breath.

"The winner of *Recipe for Success, Season Two*, is Grace Donahue!"

A chorus of cheers filled the space. Yaz stepped back to make room for her mom, who was the first to hug Grace, almost knocking her to the ground with her genuine joy. It was evident that in the week since she'd arrived, her mom and Grace had bonded like glaze on a Sacher torte. And just as sweetly. She then turned and beelined for Yaz.

"Yasu, you make me so proud! You are no less a winner for showing people what you are capable of. You are still the tiger, but more importantly, you are my baby and I love you."

"Thank you, Mom, but honestly, I'm fine. I think the judges made the right call and the experience was amazing."

"I think you ended up with a pretty good prize!" Her mom punctuated her comment with several quick looks between Grace and Yaz, eyebrows raising and lowering like a vaudeville comedian.

Yaz leaned down and planted a kiss on her mom's cheek. "I think so too."

Her mom then turned toward the crowd that was swarming Grace and, in a voice loud enough to wake the dead shouted, "How do you plan to spend your winnings, Grace?"

Yaz shot a look at her mom and rolled her eyes. She hadn't been back in Canada for even a week but had established a comfort level with Grace that apparently gave her leave to ask questions reserved for family. But Grace took it in stride. Or maybe she felt like family, Yaz thought and censured her rebuke.

"That's a great question, Okaasan." Grace nodded approvingly and smiled. "Yaz, maybe now is a good time?"

Grace took Yaz's hand and pulled her up from the couch. She reached for a bottle of bubbly and began removing the foil and unwiring the top.

"As you now know, Grace Donahue was the big winner of *Recipe for Success*." Yaz could hardly contain her pride and she lifted Grace's arm up with one hand and the bottle with the other. She waited until the applause subsided. "But the runner-up prizes were generous, additionally so because the sponsors had only three finalists instead of four, thanks to our mushroom friends." Yaz didn't feel great about benefiting from another's misfortune, but it was Brassard, after all, so she allowed herself a smile as she popped the champagne and began filling glasses. Once delivered, she popped another, offering bubbly cider to the non-drinkers.

"Kew was awarded enough cash to help out his family's business, so cheers to that." Grace raised her glass and the others joined in.

Yaz took Grace's hand and squeezed it, feeling the love and joy spread up her arm. "I was the recipient of a very nice chunk of change. Mama, sorry for telling you that it was airmiles that got you here. In addition, Kew, Grace, and I were also given an entire collection of professional kitchen appliances. So tonight, we have a couple of surprises." She turned and nodded at Grace, who took the cue.

"Sabrina. Yaz asked me to announce this because she knew she'd get all mushy. She's not as tough as she looks. In fact, she's a total softie."

A chorus of trues floated around the room. Yaz's face flushed and she jerked lightly on Grace's arm. It still felt strange to hear how Grace saw her, and even more strange to be seen.

"So, Sabrina...from what Yaz tells me, you are the reason she went as far as she did in the competition. Your mentoring gave her technical skills that elevated her cooking to exceptional levels. She would like to donate the appliances to Safe Harbor as a small way of thanking you for your encouragement, guidance, and generosity."

Sabrina's hands went to her mouth, and her eyes widened. "Oh my God," she finally managed through tears. "You know how much we need a new stove!"

Yaz went over and gave Sabrina a hug. "Well, you're getting that, and a whole lot more. We'll have to start clearing out the ancients to make space for the moderns. A truck will be pulling up next week."

Another round of bubbly was poured as the small but special group chatted about the show. Yaz overheard comments about Grace's playtime with the baby goats, which fortunately took the edge off the more serious incident in the river. Her mom had almost lost her mind with worry as she watched that episode, white-knuckled and wide-eyed.

"When are you going to make that goat milk ice cream for me, Yaz?" Jenni poked at her as her glass was refilled.

"Hold that thought, cousin. We have another little surprise for you all." Yaz rejoined Grace and the room quieted in anticipation. "I know you are all wondering what we are doing here. I mean, here, in this space." Yaz lifted her arm like Vanna White and motioned around the room they'd gathered in.

Yaz turned to Grace, who smiled and squeezed her hand. "We'd like to welcome you to what will soon be the new home of Let 'Em Meat Pie Version 2.0...to be renamed but owned and operated by Donahue and Sano."

"Or Sano and Donahue...we're still working that out!" Yaz laughed. It didn't really matter to her because the business was theirs. Together. Anticipating a few of the questions she was about to get pummeled with, she went on to explain that Grace would manage the finances, and front of house. Her generous way with people and mercilessly frugal wrangling of numbers suited the business, but Yaz insisted as they built the business plan that she would keep a heavy hand in the kitchen, helping with menu concepts and keeping her skills up. After all, viewers of *Recipe for Success* would want to taste a winner's dish.

"We know how difficult the business of restaurant ownership is, but we have a leg up. A few, actually. We're starting with an amazing location that includes a beautiful two-level apartment upstairs."

"Housewarming TBD!" Grace announced.

"We have a full set of new appliances and have already set up the kitchen. Our winnings helped to clear our debts…"

Grace raised her glass and beamed. "Cheers to that!" She'd been so much lighter since getting out from under her family's debt and was now working to build the business without their interference.

"And we are now building our team," Yaz concluded, feeling the pride deep in her soul.

"My dear daughter, who will head up the kitchen?"

Yaz could hear the expectation in her mother's voice and took a moment to collect her thoughts. She could certainly envision being an executive chef at some point, but two years as a line cook and six weeks on a televised cooking show was not a substitution for the years in the kitchen needed to earn that distinction. She and Grace both knew this. They also agreed that the menu they were building would require modifications if they wanted to provide more than a limited takeout experience. It would expand to include side dishes, appetizers, and desserts. And the mains would need to reflect the diverse community they'd chosen as their location. Yaz, even with Grace in support, had no desire to shoulder this substantive task, but together they'd agreed on a plan.

"I will not. Grace and I, as I said, are very fortunate. We have a friend who is experienced, and who is looking for new challenges in this next stage of her culinary career. Lyn Sanyal has agreed to be our consultant and executive chef for the first year of our operation."

As Lyn saluted the group, Bette raised a glass and exclaimed, "Thank God she'll be out from under my feet! The woman is bored, and she needs to follow someone else around for a while. Yaz and Grace, I hope you know what you're in for!" Bette rolled away from Lyn's spirited push in the nick of time and laughed.

"She's right. I'm bored. But I'm also really excited to help these two out. To be honest, they won't need my input for long. They are, as you could see from the show, extremely talented chefs."

"Thank you, Lyn." Grace faced the group. "I would like to make an offer to Jenni and Emily. We have a place for you on our staff if you want it. We're small, but mighty, and would be honored if you'd agree."

Yaz felt tears build as she watched Jenni and Emily fall under Grace's spell. *Who could help themselves?* Emily had proven an asset while Grace was seconded for the show and had graduated from her culinary course. Jenni, of course, felt like she'd discovered a long-lost sister in Grace. The three were kindred in their love of fashion and would no doubt bond over designing and decorating the new dining area, something Yaz was happy to leave in their capable hands if it meant she would never need to understand the myriad of differences between a Windsor and a King Louis chair, or the advantages of boucle over organic poplin upholstery. And she was good with that. *Very good.*

❖

Lyn and Bette were the last of the watch party crew to take up their coats. Grace walked them to the door, arms hooked in each of theirs, feeling the love and pride flowing between them. "Thank you so much for coming. Thanks, well, thanks for everything."

Bette spun and put a hand gently on her cheek. "Gracie, you earned it. And I should be thanking you. The competition was so close this year, and the dishes were exceptional. It could not have been a closer finale. We've already signed a deal with the network for another season."

"That's great! Let me know if we can help out in any way."

"Absolutely. Unbiased guest judges are always welcome! Babe," she turned to Lyn and winked, "I'm going to go warm up the car while you say good night to our girl here."

The door had barely closed behind her when Lyn pulled Grace into a hug. "How are you, Gracie?"

"Honestly, I'm great. I owe you."

Lyn looked puzzled.

"Your little pep talk, Lyn, was not lost on me."

"Gracie, I saw the way you cooked in that last round. I may have thrown a little pep on you, but, girl, you cooked. You. And now, well, you look...I don't know...not like your old self. I don't mean that in a bad way. Not at all. It's just that after Joss died, you looked, um..."

"Broken?"

Lyn nodded and tears welled in her eyes.

"I felt broken then. I don't feel that way anymore. And it's not because of Yaz, though she absolutely holds me together. She's amazing. And it's not even because I finally paid back every cent I owed my parents, who didn't even want it."

"No kidding. That money was their hold on you." Lyn put her hand on Grace's shoulder. "But I'm sure that as parents, they'll miss you if they don't already."

Grace wasn't expecting to hear Lyn say that. She'd never held back on her contempt for the Donahues before. "Have you changed your mind about them? What gives?"

"I'm not their biggest fan..."

"Understatement much?"

Lyn laughed. "I'm not happy about how they've treated you, but lately I've been thinking more clearly about my own experience of loss—maybe that comes with time—and I think I can afford a bit of grace with them. Small g."

Grace found herself nodding in agreement. Months ago, entertaining the notion of forgiveness where her parents were concerned would've surprised her, but she and Yaz had had many conversations lately about the loss of her dad. "Distance is probably the best thing for me at the moment, but I'm open to seeing how things play out with them now that we're on more level ground. At least, that's where I've landed for now." She shrugged and smiled.

"And where have you landed on feeling broken?"

"Well, we're back to the pep talk. It was honest, Lyn, and it was difficult. I didn't want to hear the truth then, of course..."

"Of course." Lyn squeezed her arm.

"But afterward, it was like I was able to make connections again. Between ingredients and their best qualities. Between my life and my own true happiness. Between all the things that Grannie Jean taught me, all the things that Joss taught me, and all the things that you taught me. All the connections were suddenly clear. Weird, right?"

"Not weird at all. It's called living, Gracie."

Headlights flashed through the front windows and a horn sounded. Lyn pulled her in for another hug. "I'm so happy for you. I love you."

"I love you too, Lyn."

"I hope you're still saying that once you've spent time in that kitchen with me! We'll chat menus early next week. Now go and plant a kiss on that gorgeous partner of yours."

❖

Grace finished with the last of the dishes, a task she'd always enjoyed, but now, in her own restaurant kitchen—in *their* restaurant kitchen—it felt so much more special. She was eager and over-the-moon when she considered all the possibilities of their start-up. They would rename the place, of course, because this would become so much more than a meat pie shop. And it was Yaz's place as well as hers. They'd worked hard on the business plan and the financing fell into place with the help of not only the show's prizes, but of the many friends who came forward to invest time and money into the venture. They both felt embraced by the community, and equally honored to fill the space with food and friendship. It was more than everything because love was the very foundation they were building upon.

"What are you thinking about, beautiful?" Yaz had taken a small wooden crate of oysters out of the fridge and was busily coaxing them open.

Grace couldn't help but laugh as she sidled up to her. "As a matter of fact, I was thinking about how the world is our oyster, handsome. Is it weird that we're hungry?"

"Not weird. I think we were both so focused on making sure everyone had a good time that we didn't eat much ourselves."

"Are you sure your mom is okay staying at the hotel? Jenni said she could stay in your old room at the apartment."

"You couldn't pry Mom from that hotel if you tried. You know about the late-night chocolate buffet they offer, right? And Jenni? Dollars to doughnuts she's been staying with her."

"Oh, so this chocolate addiction is a family trait, is it?"

"Likely. Fortunately, I've found something a little sweeter to sate my impulses."

Grace knew Yaz was referring to the oysters, but she nonetheless felt her breath catch, having spent the past few months becoming intimately familiar with many of Yaz's preferences. Sweet. Spicy. And pretty much everything in between. She had never felt so satisfied, indulged, and perpetually aroused in her life.

As Yaz shucked, Grace chopped a shallot and added it to some vinegar and seasonings in a bowl. She whisked the mignonette mindlessly as she admired the strength of Yaz's muscled fingers and hands as they convinced the rock-hard shells to surrender. She also noted the meticulousness with which the delicate body of the oyster was extracted from its pearly bed, then with equal care returned to the sea's brine pooled within its shell. This was Yaz. Tough yet tender. And so loved.

"I had a moment to talk to Sabrina about our plan." Grace dipped a finger in the bowl and tasted the sauce. *Perfect.*

Yaz looked up and wiped her hand with the towel she used to protect her from the danger of a slipped shucking knife. "And? Is she willing to come in as a sous chef? I know she has demands at the shelter, and maybe it won't work out, but…"

"Easy, Tiger." Grace accepted the last open oyster from Yaz and set it on the coarse salt bed. "She is going to talk to her sponsor. She almost cried when I asked, but she knows her own limits and needs to make sure she can handle the stress. And she doesn't want to give up her work at Safe Harbor, so…"

"Gotcha. I'm glad she's considering it though. That's good, right?" Yaz spooned the mignonette Grace had prepared on each of the oysters.

"It's better than good, but either way, Yaz, we're going to be alright. You are much more talented than I think you realize." *In so many ways.* "Speaking of talents, I hope you don't mind but I've planned a little something." She opened the fridge and pulled out a tray with a bottle of champagne and two fluted glasses. "Come with me, and bring your friends," she said, motioning to the tray of mollusks and heading to the stairs at the back of the kitchen, leading to their apartment.

Instead of stopping in the small eating area inside the door, Grace continued up the next flight to the bedroom, crooking her finger at Yaz to follow.

"What is this?" Yaz stopped in the doorway to their room and nodded toward the bed.

Earlier in the day, expecting that they would have time once their guests left for a private celebration, Grace had laid a red checkered tablecloth and some linen napkins on the bed. "A picnic, Tiger, as if you can't tell. But you're overdressed for it." She relieved Yaz of the tray, setting it on the night table, and stepped into her arms before unbuttoning and removing her chef's jacket. She was wearing a black muscle shirt, skintight, the way Grace loved it. Just one glance of the nipples that strained beneath it, and the tattoo tiger ever-ready over Yaz's shoulder, was all it took for her juices to flow, heat to build, and breath to quicken. It had been like this since their first night together.

"Oyster?" Yaz held the pearly bowl below Grace's mouth.

She pulled back dubiously at first, then caught a whiff of the brine and leaned in to take a deeper inhale.

"Wait a second." Yaz pulled the shucked mollusk away. "Is this your first oyster?"

Grace squinted as if she'd been challenged. "There's a first time for everything!" She snatched the shell from Yaz, careful not to spill a drop of the liquor, and threw it back like a tequila shot, hoping it wouldn't possess a similar punch.

Grace paused and considered the flavor bomb that had passed easily across her tongue and down her throat. It tasted like the sea. Cold. Creamy. Sweet but with an interesting back note that reminded her of fruit. Pear maybe? Or cucumber. The acid from the mignonette cut the richness perfectly, enhancing its briny notes. "No wonder they're considered an aphrodisiac. They remind me of, well…"

"I think so too." Yaz elbowed her playfully. "But not quite as good."

"Agreed."

"Did you know that the Pacific oyster aquaculture was introduced to this coast by Japanese immigrants like, over two hundred years ago?"

Grace ate another, this time taking an extra moment to appreciate the subtle nuance of sugar and steel that crossed her palate. "That makes oysters my second favorite treat to come out of Japan."

She fed an oyster to Yaz, then leaned in and kissed her. She let her tongue trace the soft inner side of Yaz's lower lip, and the moan it elicited caused a thrum of exhilaration from deep within. She noticed Yaz's eyes had darkened to a shade of espresso, a change Grace now knew signaled she'd become hungry for something else. She traced her fingers along the tiger's front haunches. "You know this is only the appetizer."

"I can't even imagine what's on the dessert menu," Yaz's voice had deepened, her yearning palpable, "but I'll save room."

THE END

THE END

About the Author

Annie McDonald plans to celebrate her country by writing novels set in each of her native land's ten provinces and three territories. She hopes to respectfully represent the astonishing diversity of the people who call Canada home.

Annie's second novel, *When Sparks Fly*, was a finalist for the Golden Crown Literary Association's Goldie Award in the category Contemporary Romance: Short Novels.

She writes while staring at the Atlantic blue of the Nova Scotia coastline, grateful always for her home, family, friends, and dogs Scapa and Rey. And yes, she still loves a perfect stout with a salty potato chip.

About the Author

Books Available from Bold Strokes Books

Discovering Gold by Sam Ledel. In 1920s Colorado, a single mother and a rowdy cowgirl must set aside their fears and initial reservations about one another if they want to find love in the mining town each of them calls home. (978-1-63679-786-1)

Dream a Little Dream by Melissa Brayden. Savanna can't believe it when Dr. Kyle Remington, the woman who left her feeling like a fool, shows up in Dreamer's Bay. Life is too complicated for second chances. Or is it? (978-1-63679-839-4)

Emma by the Sea by Sarah G. Levine. A delightful modern-day romance inspired by Emma, one of Jane Austen's most beloved novels. (978-1-63679-879-0)

Goodbye, Hello by Heather K O'Malley. With so much time apart and the challenges of a long-distance relationship, Kelly and Teresa's second chance at love may end just as awkwardly as the first. (978-1-63679-790-8)

One Measure of Love by Annie McDonald. Vancouver's hit competitive cooking show Recipe for Success has begun filming its second season and two talented young chefs are desperate for more than a winning dish. (978-1-63679-827-1)

The Smallest Day by J.M. Redmann. The first bullet missed— can Micky Knight stop the second bullet from finding its target? (978-1-63679-854-7)

To Please Her by Elena Abbott. A spilled coffee leads Sabrina into a world of erotic BDSM that may just land her the love of her life. (978-1-63679-849-3)

Two Weddings and a Funeral by Claudia Parr. Stella and Theo have spent the last thirteen years pretending they can be just friends, but surely "just friends" don't make out every chance they get. (978-1-63679-820-2)

Coming Up Clutch by Anna Gram. College softball star Kelly "Razor" Mitchell hung up her cleats early, but when former crush, now coach Ashton Sharpe shows up on her doorstep seven years later, beautiful as ever, Razor hopes the longing in her gaze has nothing to do with softball. (978-1-63679-817-2)

Firecamp by Jaycie Morrison. Going their separate ways seemed inevitable for two people as different as Fallon and Nora, while meeting up again is strictly coincidental. (978-1-63679-753-3)

Fixed Up by Aurora Rey. When electrician Jack Barrow and artist Ellie Lancaster get stuck on a job site during a blizzard, close quarters send all sorts of sparks flying. (978-1-63679-788-5)

Stranded by Ronica Black. Can Abigail and Whitley overcome their personal hang-ups and stubbornness to survive not only Alaska, but a dangerous stalker as well? (978-1-63679-761-8)

Whisk Me Away by Georgia Beers. Regan's a gorgeous flake. Ava, a beautiful untouchable ice queen. When they meet again at a retreat for up-and-coming pastry chefs, the competition, and the ovens, heat up. (978-1-63679-796-0)

Across the Enchanted Border by Crin Claxton. Magic, telepathy, swordsmanship, tyranny, and tenderness abound in a tale of two lands separated by the enchanted border. (978-1-63679-804-2)

Deep Cover by Kara A. McLeod. Running from your problems by pretending to be someone else only works if the person you're pretending to be doesn't have even bigger problems. (978-1-63679-808-0)

Good Game by Suzanne Lenoir. Even though Lauren has sworn off dating gamers, it's becoming hard to resist the multifaceted Sam. An opposites attract lesbian romance. (978-1-63679-764-9)

Innocence of the Maiden by Ileandra Young. Three powerful women. Two covens at war. One horrifying murder. When mighty and powerful witches begin to butt heads, who out there is strong enough to mediate? (978-1-63679-765-6)

Protection in Paradise by Julia Underwood. When arson forces them together, the flames between chief of police Eve Maguire and librarian Shaye Hayden aren't that easy to extinguish. (978-1-63679-847-9)

Too Forward by Krystina Rivers. Just as professional basketball player Jane May's career finally starts heating up, a new relationship with her team's brand consultant could derail the success and happiness she's struggled so long to find. (978-1-63679-717-5)

Worth Waiting For by Kristin Keppler. For Peyton and Hanna, reliving the past is painful, but looking back might be the only way to move forward. (978-1-63679-773-1)

Flowers and Gemstones by Alaina Erdell. Caught between past loves and present secrets, Hannah and Vanessa must each decide if the other is worth making difficult changes for a shot at happiness. (978-1-63679-745-8)

Foul Play by Erin Kaste. Music librarian Kirsten Lindquist knows someone is stalking the symphony musicians, but can she prove that a string of murders and suspicious accidents are connected, all without becoming a victim herself? (978-1-63679-689-5)

Hollywood Hearts by Toni Logan. What happens when an A-list actress falls for a paparazzo, having no idea her love interest is the one responsible for the photos in a troublesome tabloid scandal targeting her? (978-1-63679-695-6)

Ride It Out by Jenna Jarvis. When the COVID-19 lockdown traps Mick and Katy in situations they'd convinced themselves were temporary, they're forced to face what they really want from their lives, and who they want to share them with. (978-1-63679-709-0)

Scarlet Love by Gun Brooke. Felicienne de Montagne is content with her hybrid flowers and greenhouses—until she finds adventurer Puck Aston on her doorstep and realizes nothing will ever be the same. (978-1-63679-721-2)

The Hard Stuff by Ana Hartnett. When Hannah, the sales manager for a big liquor brand, moves to Alexandra's hometown and rivals her local distillery, sparks of friction and attraction fly. It turns out the liquor is the least of the hard stuff. (978-1-63679-599-7)

The Hunter and Her Witch by Rachel Sullivan. When an ex-witch-hunter falls for a witch, buried pasts are unearthed, and love is placed on trial. (978-1-63679-830-1)

Trustfall by Patricia Evans. Devri and Shiv never expect their feelings for each other to linger, but sometimes what you've always wanted has a way of leading you to who you've always needed. (978-1-63679-705-2)

www.ingramcontent.com/pod-product-compliance
Lightning Source LLC
Chambersburg PA
CBHW032213030726
47494CB00020B/1052